The
Storming

Full Disclosure Two

Ellis Logan

An Earth Lodge® Publication
Roxbury, Connecticut

Published in the U.S.A. by Earth Lodge®
Cover Design by Maya Cointreau

ISBN 978-1-944396-52-7

"Children of the stars, we have been watching you, feeling you, loving you, for eons. Watching and waiting, and we have seen your hearts. The time to seek dominion over others has passed. Love is winning."

- The Nommo

Prologue

Three days. I've been a prisoner for three days. More, if you count the time I spent knocked out and tied up on the back of my best friend's gravicycle, speeding through the air towards Valhalla.

I haven't spoken to Khai since then, although he's been talking to me plenty. I have nothing to say to him.

What would you say to the man who tased you in a bid to keep you "safe?"

Right. Exactly.

I'm free to wander Airmed's home and grounds, but if I try to leave? Let's just say that water fae can create stationary shockwaves, too, and Airmed is one of the best at shielding techniques. Someday, the ancient healer says, she'll teach me how, but not until she's sure I've come to my senses.

So, I'm stuck here.

My mother calls every night. I hear Airmed talking with her, but I won't speak to her. Right now, my voice, or lack of it, feels like my only weapon. My one form of protest.

But I get updates. David, my boyfriend, is still missing. Mialloch and Dorian have both come by to visit, representatives of the Light Council and its fae Guard. I told them everything I knew, and it didn't feel like nearly enough. I can't shake the feeling that Mialloch knows more than he's telling me. Yesterday a meeting was finally arranged with David's organization in Boston, but from what I've heard, trust levels are low between them and the fae.

I can't imagine why.

Everyone needs to work together, to save all the innocent people who have been taken. First, though, the fae and starseeds have things to discuss. Plans to make. They want to figure out just how they can help each other, what the other side can and cannot do.

Every hour that passes here makes me want to scream. How long before David gets brainwashed, before he becomes a warper?

Is he one of them already?

I can't just sit here and wait. I can't.

But I can't leave, either.

It's for my own safety, they say. I need to relax. Let the adults handle things. Never mind that I officially became an adult over a year ago.

No matter what I say, they won't let me leave. I'm to stay here and train in water magic with Airmed like a child in a nursery, while the grownups go to war.

Which is why, this evening I've made a decision. I'm going to let Airmed teach me. I'm going to smile and cooperate. I'm even going to forgive Khai. He's been offering to show me some new sparring moves: it turns out that we didn't already know everything, after all, *and Khai wants to teach me what he's learning at the Light Guard Academy.*

So, I'm going to let him. It's what friends do, right? Forgive? Forget?

I'm a quick study, and I can see that I still have a lot to learn.

And then, I'm breaking the hell out of here.

Chapter 1

"Ana, you're not paying attention."

I blinked, slowly focusing on my teacher. "Sorry."

"Honestly, Ana, you say you want to learn but your mind is somewhere else."

I clenched my fists under the table, forcing my voice to sound calm and breezy. "Yeah, I don't know what's wrong with me, sorry. I am trying."

Airmed started running on again about the importance of controlling one's emotions before beginning any sort of water magic.

That was a rich, I thought, coming from her. Really, didn't she know where my mind was?

I could have told her easily. I'd been thinking about David. Where he was, how he was, and how to find him.

The thing is, David's people had been fighting warpers for years, for millennia, even. Both groups carried the same ancient alien hybrid DNA, but while most starseeds used their psychic abilities for good, the warpers hated humans. They'd always wanted more power, but since the fae had come out of hiding and revealed themselves to the world thirty years earlier, the new world utopia had put a damper on their plans. Now humans were evolving to become more like us, the fae, and the world was filled with magic. David said there were fewer warpers these days, due in part to a human-starseed watchdog organization called the Gregors, but they still existed.

David believed a new faction we'd accidentally stumbled upon might be more dangerous than all the ones that had come before. They were building an army, mind-warping innocent starseeds, turning them into mindless evil drones dedicated to using their powers for ill. I didn't have a lot of confidence in the ability of the starseeds to find my boyfriend on their own, and the latest news I'd heard was that the Light Guards of the fae didn't want to get involved in what they saw as a starseed problem.

Fine, I thought. I had no problem with that. I understood why they didn't think it was their fight.

I, however, wanted to get involved, needed to get involved. My boyfriend's mental health, maybe even his life, was on the line. How could anyone expect me to just *sit* here?

I'd been trying to make the most of it, learning as much as I could. Airmed was a fantastic teacher, one of the best. Few fae my age could say they had met her, let alone studied with the great and powerful healer, a true Ancient at over a thousand years old and one of the most gifted water fae on the planet.

My grandmother said that I was being ungrateful. My parents understood how I felt, but refused to buckle under my emotional pleas. At least my father had promised to keep in touch with the Starseed headquarters and send me updates regularly. Too bad there was nothing to report: the trail had gone cold. It was as if the starseeds that had been taken hostage from the Gregors' headquarters in Montreal had simply disappeared. How you could hide the kidnapping of thirty-eight people in broad daylight, I had no idea, but somehow, it had been done. Surveillance footage had been scrambled. Forensic evidence was untraceable, as if the perpetrators didn't even have DNA to shed. Witnesses, neighbors who should have seen everything, acted as if they'd never even noticed the building existed.

No doubt, the warpers had used their powers to cover their tracks. The Gregors suspected the starseeds had been taken south to an off-grid facility like the one I'd found in Northern Vermont when I'd been hiking the Long Trail, but in reality it was anybody's guess.

I wondered if-

"Ana, pay attention!"

"Honestly, I am listening," I protested, squeezing out the doubts cycling in my head. "I'm paying attention, I swear."

She eyed me doubtfully, but plowed on.

"Okay, well, as I was saying, as fae much of our power comes from our emotions, our connection to the deepest part of ourselves and the elements that we have the most affinity with. For you and me, that's water, which makes our emotional state doubly important. If we don't have a handle on our emotions, our actions can become too powerful, dangerous. Having the ability to knock back an opponent without even thinking obviously would have big benefits for our survival when fae first evolved, but we aren't living in the wilds of an Ancient planet anymore. You have to watch yourself, be sure that your emotions don't get away from you in the heat of the moment. If you get too angry, if someone surprises you and you don't have a handle on your powers, you could seriously hurt someone without meaning it."

Airmed frowned, lost in thought for a moment.

"When I was still a maiden," she said softly, pulling my attention back just when my own mind was threatening to change tack, "my brother used to love playing tricks on me. One day, he jumped out at me from behind the stable, wanting to surprise me, as siblings so often will. I didn't mean to do it. I wasn't thinking. I threw up my hands and blasted him back with a wave of energy. He must have flown twenty feet across the yard hitting his head, against our home. I laughed so hard, until I realized that he had hit his head on the stones bricks behind him. It took me two days of healing to bring him back from his concussion."

"I never heard that story before."

"Yes, well, no one sang about it in the old sagas. We didn't spread the story around, it wasn't exactly inspiring. My father didn't want the other fae to know that his daughter couldn't control her power. I was ashamed for many years after that. Incidents like that were part of the reason that I hid from people for so long. I had so many years where I worried that my power might slip out, hurt somebody, do damage that I would not be able to repair. I grew tired of making mistakes, tired of having to choose sides in the war between the light and the dark."

"But you're out now. You see people now. You've returned to Aeden. You're not hiding anymore in the hills of Ireland."

"No, I'm not. With the dark gone, there are no sides to choose," she said, referring to the utopia my mother had birthed thirty years before when she awakened the powers of the Tree of Life, boosting the great red sun, Anansanna, deep within the Earth's crust, and banishing evil from the world forever. At least, that's what we'd thought had happened. How were we to know that another race of aliens existed on the planet, one that was immune to the positive effects of the flare? Somehow, that knowledge had been lost to the ages, if it had ever even existed, and they'd had thirty years to plot against our brave new world.

"No one came to seek me anymore in that land, my legends have faded with time. Few even imagine that I still live. And with so many fae gaining stronger powers now through the grace of Anansanna, you and your mother having the ability to heal, I'm not the only one anymore. Every day, new people are awakening with greater powers. I don't worry so much about being bothered. My life is quiet here, usually."

She looked at me staunchly, implying that I disturbed her sanctified existence.

"Okay, sorry," I said, sullenly. "I got it. I have to keep a tight leash on my emotions. How exactly am I supposed to do that again? I mean, you can't expect me to never lose my temper, right? And how is someone even supposed to become immune to being surprised?"

"I'm not sure I ever entirely mastered it myself," Airmed said wryly, "but it is important. I think that the martial arts training your parents have already given you is a start, but I've been talking with them and we've decided you should begin daily lessons with Khai. He's been learning some techniques for centering, Light Guard practices that are supposed to have that very effect. Their training is designed not only to strengthen resolve, but create an invulnerability to surprise, so that a Light Guard is almost impossible to catch off guard."

"Why didn't my father teach me this technique when I was young? It would have come in really handy with Hollis," I said, remembering the countless times my older brother had ambushed me when we were kids.

"Why, I imagine it's because your parents assumed that you would be an earth fae, like them. Earth fae have a natural inborne ability to remain grounded, to stay calm like a rock. It is hard to upset an earth fae but with water as your element, well... Water and fire are the two most changeable fae on the spectrum. Water takes things to heart and can get overwhelmed with feelings. Fire flares up easily but also releases and forgets what they were mad about minutes after it happened."

"So you want me to study with Khai," I asked reluctantly, backtracking to what was really bothering me. I knew we'd have to make up eventually, but I'd been content to nurse my grudge. My best friend, the boy I had grown up admiring since my birth was the same one who had brought me here against my will. He'd kept what was happening to David from me, knowing that if I knew I wouldn't have agreed to come. And then, when I'd found out, when I'd resisted, he'd tased me using his ability to harness the power of fire as lightning. To say I'd found it hard to forgive him would have been an understatement.

"Yes, Ana. It's time, don't you think? When he visits you ignore him. I know you feel like he wronged you, but he was following your family's own orders. Give your friend a chance. Can't you feel his pain?"

"His pain?" I scoffed. "What would any of you know about pain? What about how I feel-"

"That's enough," she cut me off. "I'm not going to go through this again with you. I know exactly how you feel, but I can also see how pointless it is to prolong this little feud the two of you have going right now."

"Whatever," I said, crossing my arms over my chest.

Airmed laughed, unfazed by my willful display.

"This is what I'm talking about. Emotions are tough." Airmed chuckled to herself as if I was some recalcitrant toddler, instead of a fully grown woman scheduled to start at university. So what if I had gotten my powers a little later than other fae? So what if Airmed was more than a thousand years my senior? Technically, legally, physically, I was an adult and I didn't appreciate my family and friends treating me like I was too weak or too young to follow my heart. I stared at her woodenly, refusing to debase myself further.

"Why don't you go get cleaned up while I prepare lunch? I will call you when it's ready," she said, dismissing me.

Chapter 2

My room was pitch black, its most common state. I usually just rolled out of bed and went to breakfast, not always bothering to change or shower every day. Often, after training with Airmed, I simply stumbled back into the room and went back to sleep. Sometimes, I would lay in the darkness, plotting my escape or worrying about David.

Airmed said that I was depressed but I knew the truth: I simply had no desire to try and impress Airmed with my fashion sense. I wasn't about to make her feel better about being party to my jail sentence. She didn't deserve it.

I knew my lack of effort bugged her. Her nightly beauty routines were legend. When she'd first heard that I'd be studying with Airmed, my mother had dared me to uncover the Ancient's secrets. I had accepted the challenge, but no longer planned on completing it. Why should I do anything for my mother, if she wouldn't help me?

Instead of cleaning up, I collapsed face down on my bed. Naps were my favorite form of protest since I'd come to Aeden. Airmed was too well-mannered to wake a guest, even if I was also her student.

Almost immediately, I found myself dreaming of the Long Trail. It was a beautiful day; shining sun, clear sky. Fluffy white clouds hung in the air. I smiled, singing to myself, enjoying the day, hiking the woods alone. I felt at peace in a way that I hadn't for so long.

It felt like coming home.

I heard a strange rasping noise followed by a series of clicks and looked around to see a large raven sitting in a tree nearby. It stared at me. When I made eye contact, it cawed three more times in that strange croaking way that ravens have. I cocked my head, looking at it.

"You trying to tell me something?" I asked.

The bird tilted its head to one side, let out another series of clicks and flew across the trail in front of me, heading deep into the woods to my left. I watched it fly, wondering what it wanted. Just as I had that thought, it landed in another tree, looking over its shoulder at me as if to say "What are you waiting for? Come on." Too bad I didn't have Hollis' gift of animal speak.

Feeling game, I ventured into the deep green canopy, following the bird. The Long Trail was famous for how wet and verdant it could become mid-summer. My mother had spoken many times about the years she had spent in other states and abroad, traveling with her mother to new towns year after year as she was growing up. She'd been so many places, both in her youth and later as an archaeologist, and almost all of them seemed like deserts compared to Vermont. Few places in the North American States, the trading nation spanning from Panama to Canada and Greenland, could compete with the lush fresh air of the northeast, in her opinion.

Now, as I scrambled off-trail, climbing over brambles, ducking under low-hanging branches and hopping over puddles, I remembered the time I'd spent hiking the Long Trail with my friends over the summer. There'd been this one week, before I'd realized that I was a water fae, where I'd been so miserable that I'd triggered rainstorm after rainstorm. Of course, I'd had no idea I was the cause of my own misery. The wetter I became, slogging along the trail, wet and cold day after day, the heavier the downpours became. I had finally broken down, crying, hating the water and the rain. Hollis has taken pity on me and suggested we should go off trail for the night, staying in the Inn at Stratton Mountain so that we could dry our clothes and wring ourselves out to face another day. In ironic homage to my misery, I'd been given the trail name, "Rain."

Now, under skies dry and glorious, the ever-present humidity and puddles on the ground didn't bother me. I divided my attention between the raven flitting among the trees and the hazards along the forest floor. After I climbed across an exceptionally large, downed oak tree, I had to stop to catch my breath and search for the bird. I couldn't see him anywhere. Had I lost him?

A low croak directly above me gave me a jolt of surprise and I looked up.

"There you are," I said, laughing. "I thought I lost you!"

The bird spread its wings, stepping off the branch and gliding to a spot twenty feet away where the roots of the fallen oak stood gnarled and perpendicular to the ground among a cluster of boulders. When I was little, I'd always thought that these uprooted tree bases were the most magical places, perfect for creating lean-tos and forts. I'd often left treats for tiny elementals and pixies that might have lived among the warren of roots. The raven disappeared around the tree and I followed, half expecting to discover a city of sprites.

What I saw was nothing that I'd expected. Instead of a fairy city, this was an entrance.

A shadowy door had been carved into the roots, bright white light glowing around its edges. I looked at it, puzzled. I walked back around the tree, verifying that there was nowhere the door could have led to other than into the tree. But for what? Who would have made a door into a tree trunk that was no more than 3 feet across? Large, sure for an oak, but not human-sized. The bird flew up and perched above the door, urging me on with another series of clicks and some chatter.

"You want me to go in here?" I asked, a frisson of fear going through me. The bird did not answer. Instead, it surprised me further by flying to my shoulder and gently it nuzzling my hair with its beak.

"Okay, I guess I'll do what you want," I said, thinking I must be crazy to be listening to a bird in the middle of the forest instead of running straight home.

I hooked my hand around one of the roots and pulled on the door. It swung open easily. Inside, the path looked like one of a million sterile, industrial hallways. White walls, dingy colorless linoleum and bright fluorescent overhead lighting.

"What is this place?" I asked as I stepped inside, turning to the raven, but he was gone. The door of roots had already swung shut and in its place was a metal door with a large sign on it marked "Restricted." Afraid, I turned and pushed on the door, but it wouldn't budge.

"Locked." I swore. Clearly, I wouldn't be able to leave the same way I'd come in. Feeling a bit like Alice in Wonderland, I turned and walked down the hallway, trying each door I passed. All were locked.

What sort of place was this? What had I gotten myself into? Yet again, I'd proceeded without thinking things through and now I was trapped. I hadn't seen a single person and I had no idea who had built this place or what its purpose was.

Finally, just when I felt like I'd be walking forever, jiggling door after door without success, the hallway ended at a set of double doors. You know, the kind you see in hospitals where only doctors are allowed to enter and family has to wait on the other side? The worst news had a way of coming through doors like that, but hoping I'd find some answers, I pushed the button on the wall that read "Access" and the doors swung open easily on their own.

Stepping quietly inside the doors before they closed again, I found myself in a hospital ward. Twenty or more beds lined the walls, each filled with an unmoving body. Someone groaned, forcing me to look around, and I spotted David half the room away, skin pale and sickly against the stark white of the bedsheet draped across him. He was hooked up to an IV drip, the liquid a lime green color. Ew, nothing good could possibly come from a color like that, I thought, the gross-looking medication doing a lot to explain David's ill pallor. I rushed to his bed, cupping his face in my hands.

"David! David, are you okay? Wake up, David, I'm here. Speak to me."

A nurse standing by one of the other beds looked up, smiling sympathetically at me. "He can't hear you, Miss. No use trying."

"What is this stuff he's hooked up to?"

"Couldn't say. Doctors don't tell me much. I just look after them, make sure they're clean, healthy."

"You call this healthy?" I asked, raising one eyebrow. The nurse had the good grace to blush and ducked her head.

"I do the best I can." She picked up her tray of instruments and left the room, going out a different door than the ones I had come through. I turned my attention back to David, leaning over him again.

"Come on, David. Open your eyes. Wake up. I know you can hear me." Nothing happened, but I wasn't about to give up, not yet. Doing a body scan, I sensed the medication doing strange things to his DNA while it kept him sedated. I used my healing ability, reaching deep into myself, sending him a jolt of awareness, a piece of myself.

"Wake up, David," I whispered against his ear. "Wake up." I heard his breath hitch. "It's going to be okay, David. I've got you," I said embracing him gently, my hands caressing the bare skin on his arms. I poured more healing energy into him with the intention of soothing his pain. Every cell in his body felt like hot coals, a slow burn raging through his body from whatever the medication was doing to his DNA. I focused on sending cool water through his veins, cleansing and recalibrating. Most bodies knew how to heal themselves when given half a chance. Given a boost from a healing fae like me, most sicknesses didn't stand a chance against the body's natural inclination to seek balance.

I could tell the moment the tide began to turn, my hands getting hotter and hotter as the healing energy poured through them while his body became cool. The cells were recalibrating, repairing themselves. When his hands eased their way over my hips, drawing me closer, I knew he was going to be okay. Then, his lips brushed across mine and my own healing began, all the fear and anxiety I'd been holding onto dissolving. Just like that, I knew things were going to work out. I'd healed David. I'd get him out of here.

But first, he needed to complete his healing, and I needed to enjoy this kiss. I moved my hands back up to his face, rubbing the pads of my thumbs over the stubble on his face, and gave myself over to the moment, pouring more and more healing energy into him even as I basked in the emotions I felt washing through me. Love. Relief. Respect.

By the gods, I really did love this man.

Khai was such an idiot. What did he know about the surge, anyway? I was a water fae, an empath. David could see auras and astral travel. We didn't need the surge to know what the other was feeling. We could see it. Feel it. Taste it. I lost myself in the kiss, stopping only when someone cleared their throat behind us. Jumping up, I ran a hand over my hair as I moved to stand in front of David, shielding him from whoever had entered the room.

"Ana?"

David's voice sounded strangled behind me. At least he could speak. Me? I just stood there gaping.

Before me, tapping one foot and looking exceedingly cross, was myself.

Well, not myself, obviously. It couldn't be. I was me. Wasn't I?

"What do you think you are doing in here?" The girl shot daggers at me with her vivid green eyes. "Who are you, and what do you think you're doing kissing my boyfriend?"

"Your boyfriend?" I exclaimed.

"Yes, my boyfriend," she said, emphasizing her possession. "Can't you see David needs to rest?"

"You're a glammer!" I said, realization dawning. This had to be a starseed. Glammers, or grammers, had the ability to create any holographic reality they chose.

"I am not," she said indignantly. "You are. And I don't appreciate the joke." She pushed me out of the way and rushed to David's side, gently brushing his hair away from his face. "Sweetheart, I am so sorry. We'll sort this out, don't you fret. Now close your eyes, you're still healing. Go to sleep."

As if on command, his eyes rolled shut.

"David!" I exclaimed. "David!" I tried to get to him, but men had appeared out of nowhere, holding my arms.

"You know what to do," she drawled, a sneer on her face as she watched them drag me away.

I was still struggling, chest heaving, legs tangled in my sheets, when I woke. Not in the forest, not in a tree. Not in a hospital ward or a warper facility. I was in my own bed, in my own room, in Airmed's house.

I raised the shutters, squinting against the bright, warm light. Dark blue hedges dotted with white roses rambled high around Airmed's grounds, mocking me.

The hedges were an ever-present reminder that I was trapped. Of course, it was Airmed's spells that jailed me, not the hedges, though the thorny walls of wild roses were almost as hard to get through. The fae had always used barrier spells to keep humans away from their lands, especially wherever a portal to Aeden was involved. The strongest barriers usually required the help of a Druid or two, but Airmed's were legendary. No one set foot on her property without an invitation. For hundreds of years, she'd lived as a recluse near an ancient clootie, or holy well, in Ireland. Anyone trying to sneak past her boundaries would feel an overwhelming sense of foreboding the closer they got, and if they pushed through the feeling, crossing the line, they would fall unconscious on the spot. Now, the boundaries around the portals to Aeden had been taken down, allowing humans free access to Aeden, but Airmed still liked her privacy.

After I'd arrived, she'd manipulated her home's boundaries to make them work in both directions so that I couldn't leave without her permission in the form of a small token, something she kept under lock and key. One day, she said, when I wasn't trying to escape, she would teach me how she did it.

I wasn't going to hold my breath.

A glance at the bedside clock told me that my nap had turned into a full night's sleep. Not only had I missed lunch, I'd slept through teatime and dinner as well. I sniffed my armpit and winced. Airmed was right. I really did need to clean up. The dream had made me feel dirty, contaminated, and my skin felt like it was crawling.

I picked out clean clothes, a light and airy pair of pants with a matching camisole so I wouldn't overheat, and headed to my private bathroom for a sonic shower. If I'd wanted the soothing effect of a water bath then I could have floated in the silver waters of Valhalla which would energize the body and ease worries. I was stubborn, though, so mostly I stuck with the sonic shower. I didn't want to feel better. I didn't want to be comfortable. I wanted to help David. If I couldn't do that, well, I didn't feel right basking in the luxury of Airmed's home while he was somewhere being held captive in much less comfortable conditions. A sonic shower was a Spartan convenience: a breezy blast of air, light and near indiscernible hum were all that signaled you were being cleaned. Dirt would be lifted off of my body by the waves, my skin sanitized and rejuvenated by the lights. Hair shiny and dry, everything smelling fresh. It was utilitarian and efficient, and it worked.

After showering, I dressed and ran a hand through my hair. The shower always left it springier than ever, super shiny and red. For most of my life, it had been a mousy, dull shade of red, but since my powers had awakened the color had turned vibrant, on fire with gold and copper highlights. I wasn't sure if the color was a side effect of my new powers or from my extended time on the trail walking in the sun – either way I hoped that it would stay like that.

It really accentuated the brilliant grass green of the one feature I had that took after my father. When he was young, he'd had beautiful green eyes with violet centers, but as his powers grew stronger his eyes had shifted to all purple. All my life, his eyes had been a brilliant ultraviolet purple. Secretly, I'd always wondered if my green eyes were another sign that I was mediocre, less powerful than the rest of my family. Gods, I was grateful to have finally come into my own powers, even if I was having a hard time controlling them.

Chapter 3

I was hunched over a bowl of sweet Roumkivara tsiichi nuts, energy-rich green Cala milk, and fresh violet colored strawberries when Khai sauntered into the room.

"Morning," he said, pulling out a chair and sitting down across from me.

I raised my eyebrows. "Morning."

He reached out, turning a napkin ring over in his hand several times, the only outward sign he displayed that he was nervous. Airmed breezed in and started making tea.

"Anna, you'll be studying with Khai today as we discussed."

"Great," I said without enthusiasm. She set out several teacups, dainty hand-painted affairs shaped like strange hybrid animals. The colorful set was from Elysielle, of course, like most of the best artisanal crafts in Aeden. The artist colony was a haven for creative types. Khai's mother Claire had met his father, Brenin Mirro, there, back when he was just a teenager dabbling in chalk art on city sidewalks.

Airmed laid a hand on Khai's shoulder, examining him with concern. "Are they feeding you alright at the Academy? Would you like a bowl of cereal like Ana?"

"No thanks, they feed me, don't worry. I had a big breakfast hours ago." He'd always been an early riser, unlike me. I preferred to stay curled up in bed until the sun was high in the sky, reading. Of course, here in Aeden Anansanna was always high above our heads, always shining. The great red sun at the center of the earth kept our underground world warm while it supplied the energy that kept the entire planet alive. You couldn't escape the light down here, which is why every home boasted sun shields over their windows that could easily be raised or lowered as needed. Spurred on by the Tree of Life below, the enormous bio-computer that had traveled with us from the stars as the Seed of Life to create this planet, The red sun had jump-started not only the terraforming of Earth but the creation of life both within and upon its surface. The seven golden towers of Valhalla still circled the tree to this day, remnants of the original ship in which our people had fled their dying world.

There was even a song about the trip, along with a prophecy about another Heart of Life who would save or end the world.

In a world before time
Our star was dying
Our world turned cold
While oceans boiled.
The Heart of Life
Our Queen so wise
She built a hive
So we could rise
Through stars we flew
Escaping all we knew
Till Heart opened ship
Triggering creation
Ending the trip
With earth, our station
A ship in place
Like an island in space

The seven towers
Bloomed to flower
The Heart of Life
Sang to wife
The red sun exploded
Our world encoded
Red queen giving birth
To home, our earth
In peace we'll live
In love we'll give
And when dark returns
The fate who earned
Blood Tyr and Faye
Will light the way
The Heart of Life will rise
Soft, strong and wise
To save or shade Aeden
And begin again.

Turns out, that strong and wise person had been my mom, and she'd saved everyone, shifted the whole world into the utopia it was today, thirty years ago. And I thought I had a tough life.

"Yes, I imagine they have you up early," Airmed nodded sagely.

"You bet," agreed Khai, popping a berry into his mouth from the bowl Airmed had put in the middle of the table. "You never know when they're going to wake you. I try to squeeze in sleep whenever I can. Usually, I lay down as soon as we're done with drills in the afternoon."

"You're like an old man," I said with a grin. "Falling asleep in your chair, napping on your own schedule."

Khai grinned back at me. "Yeah, well, you know, when you have people dragging you out of bed at any moment it's sort of the smart thing to do."

"Why do they do that?" I asked.

"They like us to be prepared for anything. *A real Light Guard must never be caught unawares*," he intoned in a low voice. "We must always be ready for attack, no matter how peaceful the world seems."

I laughed loudly. "You sound just like Dorian Claffsson," I said with glee, referring to the famously no-nonsense Light Commander.

"I should. He gives us a great speech at the beginning of every week. Apparently, learning how to sit through long boring lectures without moving a muscle is also a requirement for becoming a Guard. Of course, every time I find myself settling into the boredom, something crazy happens."

His words reminded me of the different reasons we both had for being here in Aeden. He wasn't even supposed to have come here. He should have been getting ready for another year at McGill University, working at a special internship my brother had arranged for him. Instead, after learning about the starseeds and the warpers, he'd given up school to come here and join the Guard. Khai said that it was important for him to be here now that he knew darkness still existed in our world. We'd both always seen the Guard as an outdated form of hyper-vigilance, unnecessary in modern times. Now, he said it meant something, that he could see how important it was to protect our families.

Protect me.

What he didn't get was that I didn't want protecting, that I would have been happier if he had stayed in Montreal and left me out of it. Finishing my cereal, I pushed the bowl away from me, a sour expression on my face.

"So the Light Guard is everything you dreamed it would be. I'm so glad. Tell me, what exactly is it you think you can teach me today?"

Khai opened his mouth to speak but was interrupted by the whistle of the tea kettle. Airmed filled our cups with flowers, honey and herbs, pouring the hot water over them gracefully.

"What's in here?" I asked. "It smells different."

"I've made something special for the two of you today, something that should help ease the learning process."

"You're drugging me so that I'll listen to Khai?" I asked with a smirk.

"No," Airmed said, disgruntled. "It has original ginkgo leaves from the city of Sibollae, a brain enhancer, honey laced with roses for goodwill, and chamomile and lochstuppa for peace."

Khai took a careful sip. "Well, it tastes wonderful, whatever is in it."

"Thank you for your trust, young man," Airmed said with a smile.

"Oh, I don't know if I trust you any more than Ana does, but my teacher says I must be open to new experiences. If you're going to drug me, I suppose this is a good opportunity to see if my faculties can still function properly under the influence."

I snickered and Airmed made a face. "Just drink your tea," she said, getting up from the table with her cup. "I'll be in the perennial greenhouse if you need me."

Khai and I waited until we heard her leave the house and then we both burst into giggles. I was the first one to sober up. He reached out a hand, taking mine in his.

"I've missed this," he murmured quietly, his bright blue eyes boring into mine. Open and honest, that was Khai.

He'd always been someone I could count on, someone I could talk to about the most serious things. My best friend Jules was great, I loved her, I did, but she didn't know what it was like to be fae. We came from different worlds. Plus, she was social and outgoing where I was quiet and studious. I'd grown up surrounded by confident, intelligent, eminently capable people. Family and friends who all moved flawlessly, ran like the winds and fought like tigers. And then there'd been me. Able, awkward Anna.

I'd always felt slightly deficient around my peers. When it had come time for my Ascension at the age of eighteen, the coming-of-age ceremony when every fae's powers were awakened, I had been eager. Ready to level up and become an earth fae like my older brother Hollis and finally be on a level playing field with Khai. But nothing had happened. Okay, I'd developed a healing ability, an uncommon power that most people envied but it wasn't what I wanted. Healing was something I could use to help other people and sure, that was nice, great even, noble. But it hadn't made me feel more capable, hadn't given me a power to counteract my brother or Khai when they thought it'd be funny to play a practical joke on me. It didn't give me the ability to grow beautiful flowers out of sand in an instant. Khai was able to shoot lightning out of his hands and light candles with his mind. Me? I'd gained the ability to heal paper cuts. Sue me if I wasn't grateful.

After over a year of waiting, I'd started to think that maybe I wouldn't ever get an active power. My father was half human, so it could happen. I knew he worried that somehow my deficiency was his fault and that killed me, you know? It really did. So when we were all hiking on the Long Trail a few weeks ago and my water powers finally awakened my first feeling had been one of pure joy and excitement. I'd been ready for this all my life. Receiving an official invitation to train with Airmed had been like a dream. Then David had been taken, and what I wanted changed.

I guess the part of me that was a healer was stronger than I knew, because all I could think about day after day was making things right for him. The thought of someone I loved being in pain hurt me more than any physical injury I'd ever had.

I shook off Khai's hand and stood up, putting my dishes in the sink with a clatter. "We should get started, don't you think?"

I turned, a smile pasted on my face. Khai looked at me, cocking his head as he tried to figure me out. I could tell he was frustrated because I knew his tell: thumb and forefinger tugging on one of the dark, short curls of hair behind his ear.

"Fine," he said, after a long pause, pushing away from the table to stand. "Airmed has a great meditation garden, let's start there."

We walked outside, Khai leading the way confidently. Airmed's home in Valhalla spread over one domed story, like most houses for those who did not live in one of the seven towering golden spires surrounding the tree of life at the city's center. The simple geodesic home sat like a golden bubble within its neat lawn and gardens on the outskirts of Valhalla, boasting several bedrooms, a library, kitchen, healing room, two bathrooms and a study. Outside, Airmed had extensive gardens as well as three large greenhouses where plants that needed cooler temperatures than the near constant eighty-five degrees of Aeden resided. Most of my training took place within the confines of her the lawns, surrounded by the hateful rose hedges.

"Ladies first," Khai waved a hand towards the entrance of the labyrinth Airmed maintained at the center of her gardens. The walking meditation was formed by tall flowers creating a spiraling path inwards that was supposed to lead to enlightenment, or something like that. I rolled my eyes at him and trudged forward, walking between the chest-high gladioli.

It wasn't easy for me to stay grumpy walking among some of my favorite flowers. The beautiful grass-like plants were heavy ladders of ascending blooms. Airmed had told me she rotated the flower crops and was currently growing some fiery-hued succulents in the greenhouse for transplantation in a few weeks, but I liked the gladioli far better. It was easy to see how the plants had gained the nickname "Sword Lily", with their tall, upright stalks piercing the air. Right now, the blooms shone gleaming white and the palest pink against gorgeous turquoise stalks of thin leaves.

Airmed had taught me that a gladiolus was one of the most high-vibrational flowers around. The remedies that she made with them allowed people to channel the energy of Anansanna more clearly. If somebody was having a hard time using their powers, gladiolus could help by strengthening their elemental connection. Her elixirs had been standard issue for Light Guards back in the days of our war with the Dark Fae. A Guard could take a few drops of her flower elixir before battle and be confident that his powers would be working at their strongest levels.

When she first told me this to me I found the information interesting, but also a bit disappointing. Upset, I had blurted out my first thought.

"Why didn't my parents think to give me some of this elixir when of my powers didn't manifest? As former

Guards, my father and grandfathers must have all known about how to use it."

"Oh child," she had said. "Do not blame them. They did come and talk to me but after a long discussion we all decided that it was in your best interest to wait. Your father had wanted to give it to you only a few months after your Ascension, but I thought we should wait until after you'd studied healing with me. I believe it's important to trust in the ways of the Gods. I've never been convinced that it's a good idea to push somebody to ascend before they are ready. Without the threat of the Dark hanging over us, I believe it is better to let nature take its course. And see? It all worked out in the end, you have your powers."

"But you didn't know how it would work out." I admit, I'd whined. "You gambled. You gambled on me!"

"Giving you the elixir would have been a gamble, as well. It can have unpredictable effects when used as a catalyst. If the Ascension ceremony is not enough to awaken a young fae's powers, who am I to push the process along? Who knows what could have happened? You might have flooded your whole house, or an entire village. Best to be cautious, I say. When you've lived as long as I have-"

Upset, I'd interrupted her. "But I haven't. No one has. Who do you think you are to decide for me? Someone should have given me the choice. No one asked me my opinion."

"You're right," she'd said, looking chagrined. "We should have asked you. As an Awakened, you are an adult. Your family should have treated you as such."

Infuriated, I'd stormed off to my room, not coming out until the following day.

Remembering the conversation now, I reached out and plucked a white flower, examining it in my hand. It was a simple bloom – six petals, ruddy pollen coated stamen at the center. So beautiful, yet simple. Why couldn't life be like that, too? I tucked it behind my ear, thinking maybe some of its peaceful nature would rub off, or at least help me learn whatever it was Khai planned to teach.

Chapter 4

By the time I reached the center of the labyrinth, I felt more relaxed, more open to whatever was going to happen. Having traveled inward with the spiral path, I felt at peace with the outer world. I was here and I was going to learn something. That was all.

The center of the garden was shaped like a starburst, rays of yellow zinnias radiating out in points from a ten-foot wide circle paved with smooth iridescent glass pebbles. The first time I had walked the labyrinth, I had expected the stones to be hot to the touch. Anansanna shone on them twenty-four-seven. Airmed had told me that the iridescent coating allowed the glass to remain at a constant temperature, matching the ambient heat of the air so that they did not burn. The bed of stones was so thick and deep that you could bury your feet like it was sand at the beach.

I sank down onto the pebbles, folding myself in a lotus position.

"Okay." I smirked up at Khai, feeling relaxed. "Teach me your wisdom, oh Master."

Khai looked down at me, an expression on his face I couldn't remember ever having seen there before. It reminded me of Hollis, the way my brother was always so calm and detached. Ever since he'd reached middle school, Hollis had been like one of my teachers at school, always playing it cool unless he was pulling some terrible prank.

"Stand," Khai said evenly.

I scrambled to my feet, clasping my hands behind my back.

"Better. Stand with your feet shoulder-width apart. Hands at your sides. Face forward. Hold your chin level, eyes forward."

"I feel like I'm in boot camp," I said, teasing again.

Khai ignored my humor and moved on through the lesson.

"Close your eyes," he ordered and I could practically feel him nod in approval as I complied. Faintly, I could hear him moving around me, walking in a circle as he spoke, the glass pebbles shifting beneath his feet. "I want you to breathe in, then out. Slowly. Make each breath last. Focus on my voice. Focus on your breath. Let the sound of my voice wash over you as you relax. Feel your feet sinking into the ground."

"That's not hard," I said, unable to stop myself, wiggling my toes and feeling the glass marbles rolling over my feet.

"Quiet," Khai ordered, his voice sharp.

Right. This was no-nonsense Khai. *Commander Khai on deck*, I thought barely stifling a giggle.

"Feel your feet sinking into the ground," he repeated. "Feel yourself sinking in. Imagine yourself like the tall straight trunk of a tree. Heavy on the Earth, straight and secure. Immovable with your roots going deep, deep down. Your spine like a steel column. Unbendable. Unbreakable. Unshiftable. Feel the light of Anansanna flowing in through the top of your head, following that steel pole, going right through you, electrifying you with a current of power that flows straight down the core of your body, into the ground. Immeasurable and inexhaustible, this is the power of your core. When your core is running this electricity, nothing can put you off balance. Nothing can stop you. The full power and glory of Anansanna flows through you. Take some time now to feel it."

I had started the exercise laughing and making fun of Khai, but his words had ignited something within me. I was able to visualize pure gold and red sparks of light coming down from Anansanna, fueling me, filling my aura, running down through my body to spill over onto the glass pebbles beneath me.

I could feel it.

I could feel the power. More than that, I could *see* the power. I could see the auric energy of everything that surrounded me, all around. Even though my eyes were closed, I could see Khai's energy field just behind my right shoulder. I could see the auras of the yellow zinnias jiggling with joy, just as I could see the energy of the gladioli – everybody was right they were high vibration plants. Their auras must have extended eighty feet into the air, exploding like fireworks. I'd never seen anything like it.

Since my emergence as a water Fae, I'd had several experiences seeing other people's auras and picking up on emotions. Being water fae made me an empath, allowing me to feel these kinds of things, but I'd had no idea that I would be able to see things on this level. The sight was both awe inspiring and a little frightening.

Khai had moved to stand in front of me. I could feel him looking at me. No, more than that, I could *see* him looking at me. Tendrils of his aura reached into mine, as if it was examining me. Exhilarated by this new ability to see, my breathing sped up.

"Relax, Ana you're going to lose the connection. Stay centered," Khai said quietly.

"No," I murmured. "I'm not going to lose anything. This is... This is unbelievable."

"Really, you think you've got it, do you?"

I nodded, eyes still closed. Who needed them? What I was seeing was more beautiful than anything I'd ever viewed in my life.

"Alright then," he chuckled. "Let's see."

He walked around me a few more times and then he reached out. Probably, he intended to push me off balance, but before he could even come close to laying a hand on me I blocked him. In one slick movement, I grabbed his wrist and spun, twisting his arm behind him. Only then did I open my eyes.

"Betcha didn't you see that one coming, did you, Khai?"

"How did you do that?" he asked.

"I saw you coming from a mile away."

"Impossible."

"No, not impossible. You're a better teacher than you know." I released his arm, coming around to face him, barely restraining myself from doing a little victory dance. "I saw everything you did, even with my eyes closed."

"But how?" he asked again, rubbing his wrist.

"I saw your aura. Everything's aura, really."

"I didn't know you could do that," Khai said

"Neither did I. I mean, I've seen auras before, I guess it's a water fae thing, but no one ever mentioned I'd be able to do this. And here I was feeling sorry for myself because

I didn't get my parent's ability to see in the dark. But I can! I can see everything, even better than they can, I bet!"

"But I don't understand. Your eyes were closed. How could you see anything at all?"

"I guess it's part of my water powers, you know, being able to pick up people's emotions and energies? Airmed never said anything about it, though."

"Maybe it's not something every water fae can do," Khai mused.

"Maybe. Airmed's focused on healing her entire life, not fighting. I bet it's just not something she's ever needed to use."

"Interesting. Let's try something." Khai pulled off the silky thin tank top he'd been wearing and walked behind me. "Close your eyes."

"Really, Khai, a blindfold? I feel like I'm in some cheesy 20th century movie."

"Yes, really. It will help you concentrate, without having to worry about keeping your eyes closed. We did this once at the academy to help us develop our other senses in case our opponent blinds us temporarily, or worse. Barit says it's all part of being prepared."

"Barit?"

"My instructor. Anyway, I was awful at it. Turns out fire fae are pretty terrible at slowing down their minds."

"What about the water fae in your class, how did they do?"

"Not much better. But it was before we learned how to center ourselves, so maybe they'd be better at it now. I don't know. There aren't actually a lot of you in the academy, I guess most water fae aren't into fighting."

"Makes sense. There's not much motivation when you can feel how scared your opponent really is."

"Right," he agreed. Tugging on my blindfold to make sure it was secure. "Can you see anything?"

"Not a thing. Even the auras are gone."

"Okay, take a moment to get back into that mindset, and we'll start. You have thirty seconds."

"Thirty seconds, that's not-"

"Twenty-five."

I cursed and spread my feet apart, falling into horse stance with my hands arms relaxed and ready in front of me, palms ready to strike.

I reached for the sun, pulling the sparkles of light into me.

"Ouch!" Khai's hand smacked me on my left shoulder, jolting me out of the meditation.

"Come on, Ana, concentrate."

"Give me a second, okay?"

Khai didn't answer, and I took his silence as permission to continue. I tried to concentrate, ignoring the sound of his feet shifting stones as he prowled around me in circles.

The light began to flow into me, igniting tingles down my spine. I almost had it, just one more second and I would be there.

A jolt of electricity spiking through my right hip made me jump.

"Dammit, Khai!" He'd shocked me, just a bit of static, but still.

Frustrated, I spun, lashing out with a roundhouse kick. I heard, rather than saw, him leap out of the way. His laughter was rich, which only pissed me off more. Angry, I stomped my foot and opened myself up to the earth and sun. The sparkles turned into a red river of energy, flooding my cells. The world burst into color around me, blinding at first in its radiance, and then coalescing into recognizable shapes and energies.

I'd done it. I had this.

I didn't have a moment to gloat, however, because Khai was coming at me again. He'd used my moment of distraction to move back towards me, dropping down so that he could swipe my legs out from under me with one foot. Just as he was about to connect, I launched myself into a Lasair round-off, curving my body as I twirling over and around him. I came out of the uniquely fae martial arts move, something capoeira strove to imitate but fell slightly short of doing, and slapped his head gently from behind.

Khai didn't speak, but I saw his aura grow brighter with excitement. He answered with a Lasair move of his own, rolling and dancing towards me as he executed a dizzying series of kicks. I managed to evade each one, but just barely. If I hadn't trained with my parents and their friends – Lasrach warriors, each of them fully trained in the Ancient specialized fighting style – I would have been doomed. As it was, I knew Khai was holding back a little. He'd trained with the same people I had, been Hollis' main sparring partner for almost two decades. They both had a natural grace that I'd rarely been able to match.

We entered into a silent dance, the only sound in the labyrinth that of the stones rasping beneath our feet. The longer it went on, the less Khai held back, aiming blows at my body with fierce determination. I could see from his aura that he was enjoying this. He started lacing his moves with small bursts of sparks and pockets of heat, so that I didn't just have to avoid Khai, I had to sidestep over red-hot stones. Just as I would move one way to avoid his fist, an arc of electricity would shoot out from his other hand. If I hadn't had the auric sight, I would have received a nasty shock. Instead, I rolled to the ground and sprang up behind him, reaching out and locking him into a Glima hold. Glima wasn't standard issue for Light Guards in Aeden, but it was something my mother had been taught from an early by her own mother. The old Viking wrestling style was designed to take your opponent down quickly and efficiently, especially when mixed with a little Krav Maga.

Touching Khai, I could both feel and see his intentions, almost as if they were my very own. I knew exactly what he was going to do before he did it. Every twist and pull he made, I countered before he could finish. In seconds, I had him pinned on the floor, his head locked between my legs while I twisted his arm in a most uncomfortable way.

I could feel him summon the lightning again, intending to stun me and use the time to extricate himself. I couldn't believe he would actually do it, though, and steeled myself the only way I knew how. I opened myself further. Could I take the energy in, the same way I was using the flow from Anansanna? There was only one way to find out. Water channeled electricity, right?

Bring it, I thought. *I can take this.*

Then, the jerk actually went for it. He placed his free hand around my leg and tased me. I softened myself, opened completely, imagining myself to be a deep pool of water, my spine a central pole, a lightning rod in water. I let the electricity in, the prickly heat of it traveling along my bones, splashing out through my skin. I pulled the energy from him, taking all of it, and gave it back ten-fold.

Khai yowled in pain, shuddering, and I released him, rolling away to spring up to crouch several feet away. He sprawled out on the ground, not moving. Worried, I ripped the blindfold from my eyes, only to see him grinning up at the sky like a maniac.

"So, that's what it feels like." I wasn't sure I'd ever seen him quite so happy.

"Are you okay?" His chest was heaving like he'd just run a marathon. Had I burned out some of his brain cells?

"Okay? That was awesome! Ana, that was amazing. I can't wait to see you take down Hollis."

"Take down- Jesus, Khai, I was worried about you! Didn't that hurt?"

"Sure it hurt. But I totally deserved it." He rolled over on his side, eyes gleaming with unshed tears as he looked at me. Tears of pain or happiness, I wondered? "What about you? Are you okay?"

"Of course I'm okay, you idiot. Don't I look okay?"

"You do. You look more than okay. You look... radiant. How did you do that, turn my power back on me?"

"I knew what you were about to do, somehow, and I just opened myself up to it. You know that old story about that sword, Excalibur, and the Lady of the Lake?"

"From King Arthur? The water elemental who gave him the magical sword?"

"Yeah, that one. I imagined I was the lake, with that sword deep inside my body, channeling all your energy."

Khai looked at me with respect. "Well, it worked. And it hurt like hell."

"Sorry, I guess you'll have to be more careful about who you tase in the future."

"It wasn't the tasing that hurt so much. It was the feeling of you ripping the power from me. You took a lot more than I was planning on giving. It felt like my soul was being ripped out of my body."

Horrified, I gaped at him. "Oh my gods, I am so sorry, Khai! I never meant to let it go that far."

"Don't sweat it, seriously. I'm fine. To be honest, I'm glad. I've been so worried about you lately, knowing you can do something like this really takes a load off."

"It does?" I wrinkled my nose at him as I reached down to help him stand.

"Definitely," he said, placing his hands on my shoulders. "You're amazing."

I blushed and he coughed, taking his hands off me. "I mean," he said, running a hand through his hair, "what you did was amazing. Who knew that seeing auras could be a superpower?"

"I know, right? David can see auras, too. I wonder if the things I see are what it looks like when he travels in the astral realms."

Khai's left eyebrow lowered, the way it always did when he didn't like something.

"What?" I asked, shrugging defensively. "I can't even mention him now?"

"Honestly? I'd rather you didn't. Every time I think about the danger he put you in I-"

"Oh my gods, seriously? You're joking, right? You know that none of this was his fault, right? I mean, he was just hiking the Long Trail to find his cousin after she went missing. How was he supposed to know Clarise's friends were warpers and that they had some obscure camp hidden in the woods for brainwashing starseeds? I mean honestly, Khai. You of all people should know that sometimes things just don't go the way you planned. And if anyone put me in danger this summer, it was me. I'm the one who insisted David not tell any of you about what was going on after I'd rescued him from the warpers in the woods. I wanted to finish the hike, and I realize now I was being stupid, but David never did anything wrong. He's a good guy, you know he is."

"He's an idiot," Khai ground out. "I never would have let you-"

"Let me? Let me?!" I groaned in frustration. "You are impossible! You just can't stop being, being, ugh, I don't know, YOU!" I shouted the last word at him, and as I did an auric shockwave of emotion blasted from my body, my chi literally shoving him backward two feet.

"You never had a problem with who I was before," he said bitterly.

"Well, I do now. You just can't stop thinking of me like a useless little girl, no matter what I do." I shook my head, backing away towards the exit. "I'm done here."

I turned and stalked off through the labyrinth, a less than satisfying path towards the house since I had to pretend I couldn't hear him following me out along the spiral.

Just as I made it to the house, Khai grabbed me, spinning me to face him.

"Look, I'm sorry, okay Ana? I don't think you're useless, I never have. I don't know where you got that idea, because it just isn't true. I can't help it if I want to keep you safe. We're like family. The thought of you being in danger makes me crazy, I can't help it."

I shook his hand off my arm, glaring straight up at him. He was much taller than me, and we were standing so close together it made my neck hurt. Annoyed, I stabbed him in the chest with my finger, forcing him to step away.

"Back off, Khai, I mean it. I care about David, and it's time you just accepted that. If you really think of me like family, then you'd better start thinking of a way we can help David, because like it or not, he's in my life now."

"In your life? He's not even here."

"And whose fault is that? It's not like he said, ooh, hey, warpers, come and kidnap me, please, I'm over here! No. That didn't happen. And now, our "family" is dragging its feet to save him because he's not fae. Well, I'm not okay with that. I'm not okay with being treated like some glass doll that needs to be kept safe. I want to be out there, finding him. I need to. If it was you or Hollis, I'd feel the same way. Why can't you all see that?"

"I just don't see how you could care so much about a guy you barely know. You only spent, what, two weeks with him, at most?"

"So?"

"So? He's not fae. He'll never really get you. You'll never be able to connect with him the way you could with another fae, you know that right?" Khai asked, sounding genuinely pained. "He'll never live as long as you because he's a starseed. You said it yourself – the starseeds are immune to the effects of Anansanna. You'd be better off with a human, at least they are beginning to show signs of longer lifespans and gaining fae abilities. He'll be dead in seventy years, tops. Where will that leave you?"

"Wow, I never knew you were such a racist, Khai," I answered bitterly.

"Me? Don't make me into something I'm not. I'm just pointing out the facts. I don't want to see you hurt, Ana. That's all I've ever cared about."

I knew he had a point but the part of me that loved Romeo and Juliet, the part that loved Jane Austen and all the old romances, that part didn't want to hear anything he had to say.

"You know what? I feel sorry for you, I do. You're so busy being *realistic*," I said, invoking sarcasm with some heavy-handed air quotes, "that you're missing the point. I could marry the most amazing fae today, and he could die in some tragic accident tomorrow. Love can't last forever. We need to hold on to it whenever we can."

"Are you actually saying that you're in love with this guy?"

"I guess I am," I acknowledged. It was the first time I'd said it out loud. "I'm in love with David. It is possible, you know, without the surge." I rolled my eyes, highlighting how ridiculous I thought the whole thing was as I referred to the epic connection that some fae were able to feel when they met their true mate. In the past, the surge had been rare, the sort of true love fairytale that most fae girls dreamed about. When people experienced the surge, they felt every emotion the other person felt. It was a connection that verged on telepathy. My parents called it *telempathy* and were sickening sweet to watch together, like most people who had the surge. Since the flare, the surge could sometimes be ignited at will between fae, and even some humans. David, being a starseed, was immune to the flare, which meant the surge could never happen with him. But people had been falling love for eons without the surge. I certainly had. So what if it wasn't perfect?

Khai's azure eyes flashed, flickers of lightning flaring through his pupils.

"Fine. It's your loss. Just don't expect me to pick up the pieces when this love of yours breaks you."

"Fine," I said, shocked by his frosty tone. I could feel his emotions, and they left me utterly cold, shivering inside with an aching sadness I couldn't define. "I won't."

"Great. Good. Perfect." Khai delivered the words like punches. He brushed his hands off, shuttering his expression. "I have something I just remembered I need to do. Tell Airmed I couldn't stay for dinner after all."

How could I tell him that suddenly I'd lost my appetite? I hated fighting with Khai. He was like a brother. A part of me. Losing the easy friendship we'd once had was like losing a limb. Part of me still felt its ghostly presence, but when I checked, nothing seemed left but cold, dead space between us.

It hurt.

Chapter 5

That night I dreamt of the forest again, the dream starting the same way: The Long Trail, the strange door hidden in the roots of a tree, the hospital, and David lying in bed. Again, I healed him with my powers. Again, we embraced, warm feelings of relief and love flowing through me from him while I continued to channel healing energy into his body. The embrace turned romantic, evolving into a kiss, the feelings flooding me becoming and more intense.

His emotions hooked me, reeled me in deeper, even as he pulled me closer. Responding to his passion I moved my body to lie next to his, reveling in the feel of his long torso against mine, his incredibly strong hands running up and down along my spine. I ran a hand through his short, thick hair. Except he couldn't have short hair. David's hair was shaggy, always falling in his eyes. His scruffiness had been part of his appeal. I loved its juxtaposition against his dependable personality, his clean-cut demeanor as a mayor's aide in Philadelphia.

I propped myself up on my elbows, examining the person beneath me and gasped in irritation.

"Khai! What are you-? How-?" He started to chuckle and I punched him in the shoulder, starting to climb off of him.

"Come on, you know you liked it," he said with a grin.

"I liked it because I thought I was kissing David, not because I was kissing you, you turd." At this, he began to laugh uncontrollably, the sound turning into a rasping, choking wheeze. I'd never heard Khai laugh like that before and I worried something was seriously wrong with him. Concern overrode irritation as I peered down into his eyes. "Are you okay? You're not acting like yourself."

I was still straddling him, sitting squarely on his hips.

"I'm fine. Great. Now that you know who I am, let's try this again." He sat up and started kissing me again, mashing his lips against mine.

"Back off," I growled, outraged. I leapt off the bed in one smooth move, ready to give him a piece of my mind. I was deciding exactly what I wanted to say when hands grabbed my arms, holding me in place. Khai started laughing again, the sound still grating horribly on my nerves.

"Take her away," he said, once he'd regained some composure. I twisted, trying to free myself from the strong arms that held me, staring at Khai as his form morphed yet again, this time into that of someone I did not know. Pasty-faced, male, with a shaved head.

"Who the hell are you?" I asked, shocked.

"No one you need to be concerned with. What you need to focus on is leaving David alone, staying out of his mind. His emotions are confused enough as it is. He doesn't need a little girl like you bothering him. You hear me? Forget about David. He's no longer your concern."

"What have you done with him? Where is he?" I didn't wait for an answer, raging on instead. "I promise, I'm going save him. And then, I'm coming for you."

The man brayed, finding my threat the most hilarious thing in the world. He shook his head as if it was just too much to take in.

"I can't, even. This girl-" he laughed, red in the face. He waved his hands, gesturing towards the door, and without a word the faceless men holding me dragged me away.

I woke up, fighting the sheets in my bed, screaming David's name.

Where was he?

Was I dreaming true, seeing something real? Or had it all been a figment of my subconscious? Staring up into the darkness of my room, I knew there was only one way to find out. I had to figure a way out of here, soon.

Chapter 6

It had taken time, but Airmed had finally decided to allow me off the premises to visit a nearby forest with Khai. Deep indigo-colored acorns had begun their annual descent, and Airmed wanted the tannin-rich nuts. So far, it seemed like more acorns had fallen on my head than into my basket, but I wasn't complaining. I was out of the house. Out of the gardens.

I was practically free.

"Those trees really have it in for you, Ana." Khai knelt nearby with a basket by his side, engaged in the same task as me. I curved my lips, pretending to smile back, when in fact on the inside I was seething.

The uncertainty of David's situation had kept me up again the night before. At least I hadn't had another dream about Khai. Talk about awkward. The truth was I had no idea what David was going through. I had no way of knowing if my dreams were just nightmares, or real visions of David's circumstances. Who knew what sick mind games the warpers were playing right now. If he was lucky, he was at some research facility getting poked with harmless needles, having his blood drawn like he said the warpers liked to do for their experiments, trying to amplify their own powers. Or maybe he was just in a holding cell somewhere, getting softened up mentally before the real games could begin. In my weaker moments, I hoped for that. The alternatives, that David might be broken or dead already, were too much to bear.

Airmed was sympathetic to my feelings. As an Ancient, she knew what it was like to lose loved ones. Ever practical, she didn't bother with hopeful platitudes, never hinted that she believed David would ever be recovered. Instead, she encouraged me to focus on my studies, to learn everything I could about healing and harnessing my water powers.

Needless to say, I'd been finding it hard to concentrate on my lessons. Any time I tried to talk to Khai about how I was feeling, it only made things worse. Our friendship already strained, I could not stomach hearing about his unjustified disapproval one more time. He claimed he didn't want to see me hurt, but that's what happened every time he frowned with condemnation. Now when he came to train with me, we limited our conversation to talking about what we were each learning. I'd asked him to show me a few things he'd learned but he hadn't, it was like he couldn't even bring himself to spar with me anymore, something we'd done together since we were small children. Once when I pressed him to run through something other than the tame balancing techniques we'd been practicing, he'd brushed me off, saying he didn't want to hurt me. I found his estimation of my abilities almost as infuriating as his censure of David.

I had trained in both human and fae martial arts for just as long as Khai. Well, nearly as long, considering I was a year and a half younger than him. True, maybe I wasn't quite as coordinated as him or my brother, or even Jules who'd been my school's star athlete, but I could hold my own.

I didn't see how refusing to teach me something new was ever going to be to my benefit and I told him so. That day, we hadn't parted on good terms. The next morning he came back with an armful of raw honey for Airmed to play with in her laboratory and a new poetry anthology from the artist's colony of Elysielle for me.

I'd pretended to be won over and gushed over his peace offering. I guess my ruse had worked, since today we'd finally gone on an outing. Keeping an eye out for any opportunity to escape, I kept missing Khai's conversational cues.

I was tired of playing games. I was tired of pretending to be happy when I wasn't and more than anything I was tired of fighting with Khai. Feeling betrayed by someone I'd always trusted and loved was exhausting. I simply had nothing left to say. I was even starting to get tired of plotting. Maybe that was the reason Airmed and Khai had decided to let me out of the house. I wondered if they could see the defeat in my eyes. Did it show in the way I walked? Because no matter how hard I thought about it, I hadn't been able to come up with a foolproof plan for getting to the earth's surface, never mind actually locating David.

Sure, I could run away and walk through Aeden, but it would take me days, maybe even weeks, to reach a portal that would take me top side. I'd never traveled through Aeden on foot, but I knew it was vast. Not only would such a long trip increase my chances of getting caught, I worried that David didn't have that kind of time.

My dreams had gotten more intense, scarier. Maybe it was just me, my subconscious fears coming to life during the dreamtime, but I couldn't shake the feeling that things were getting more serious for David. Time was running out, I knew it. I needed to escape, which meant I needed access to a gravicycle. Even one of the Fleet, the ancient unicorns who lived below Middle Earth, would do. Gravicycles were numerous in the city of Valhalla where I was being kept prisoner but they were kept under lock and key now under the orders of my grandfather, Bran Le Fay. He wasn't the Light Commander anymore but the guards of Eden still listened to him. And, of course, the Fleet were nowhere near Valhalla, roaming almost exclusively among the plains to west in Roumkivara. I had my own bonded Fleet back home, but that did me no good here.

Still, I knew I couldn't give up. Who knew when I would be allowed out again? I needed to give it a shot. I owed it to David.

Dropping another acorn into my basket, I looked over at Khai. His basket looked much fuller than mine, no surprise considering how little attention I'd been paying to the chore. Picking up a heavy rock in my hand, I stood up, dusting myself off and looping my basket over my other arm.

"I think we should call it a day, I'm tired of being attacked by trees." I shrugged, giving him a feeble smile.

"Alright. I think between the two of us we've collected enough anyways," he said, gesturing towards two more baskets standing heavy with nuts at the base of another tree. "Here give me yours and I'll empty it into the other three, that way you'll only have to carry one back to the house."

"Thanks, Khai," I said sweetly, watching him bend over to pick up my basket. I held my breath, feeling guilty about the pain I was about to cause him. Then, before I could lose my resolve, I raised my hand and swung my fist down towards his neck, cracking the stone against the base of his skull. Khai fell down, out cold on the ground. Quickly, I knelt down, assessing his life force. The healing power in me wanted to rise up, bring him back to consciousness, but I tamped it down, denying any action that would interfere with my plan. I did a quick body scan and could tell he was okay. Without my interference, he'd probably sleep for thirty minutes, which gave me just that much time to get out of the forest, find some transportation and ride away from Valhalla. A twinge of guilt washed over me but I reminded myself that I couldn't risk waiting any longer. David needed me.

I placed a small kiss on the side of Khai's head. "I'm sorry, Khai. I hope you'll understand. I would do the same if it was you out there."

And then, I ran.

I actually did have a plan, even it wasn't the greatest. On our walk to the forest, we'd passed a small farmstead. A sister and brother had been playing in the yard, taking turns on a small golden disc the size of a large pizza. Instantly, I had recognized the hoverboard, a common child's toy in Aeden. When I was a kid I hadn't been much of a boarder; I'd fallen off a lot more than I'd stayed on. My coordination was only marginally better than it had been when I was younger, so I wasn't sure I'd be able to stay on the thing. Even so, it seemed like my best shot at the moment, despite the fact that it was a lot slower than a gravicycle which could do upwards of 200 miles an hour.

So yeah, maybe my plan wasn't the best. My only chance was if everyone wasted time, a lot of time, assuming I'd go to Valhalla first and searching for me there.

As I ran through the woods, rust-colored light filtering through the dark azure leaves above, I couldn't help feeling like I was in one of those terrible old war movies that we used to watch in Global History class. An old song came to mind, the memory crooning in my ear. *Better run through the jungle, run through the jungle.* The upbeat tune made me feel crazed, pushing me along, and I had to stop myself from laughing. *You're hysterical, Ana. Calm down. Just run.* I wasn't in a jungle, not really. There weren't any dangerous panthers, snakes or monkeys to watch out for and certainly no dangerous enemies. The only thing I had to worry about here in Aeden was running into the people who cared about me too much, people who thought that my safety was more important than David's.

I forced myself to relax, breathing in and out in a regular rhythm as I ran. Hysteria wouldn't help anyone. I imagined myself balanced and strong, like Khai had been teaching me. Centered. My mind cleared, and I spent the next several minutes preparing a whole story to convince the kids to lend me their hoverboard.

I needn't have bothered. When I reached the farmstead, no one was in the yard. As far as I could tell, no one was home. Maybe they had gone into the city to sell things, or maybe they were in the fields, I didn't know, but leaning against one of the golden dome sheds was the hoverboard.

I steeled myself, preparing for what I was about to do. I was taught well by my parents never to steal, never to lie, never to harm anyone except in self-defense. Already, I had lied to people I cared about, and hurt Khai in cold blood. I'd apologize for it later, but I didn't feel that guilty. I wasn't sure if that made me a bad person or not, but stealing some kids' hoverboard I felt like I'd fallen pretty low. Quickly, I said a prayer of thanks and apologies, vowing to myself that I would return the board to them someday, or get them something even better.

It was now or never.

I grabbed the board, running my fingertips along its edge, trying to remember where the tiny button was on these things that turned it on. The hoverboard worked along the same lines as the gravicycle, relying on Ancient anti-gravity technology from our ancestors. Tiny propulsion jets ran along all sides of the board. By leaning one way you could change direction, and the more weight you put on your toes when you leaned the faster you would go, although most of the steering was done with your hips and your knees. Like I said, I'd spent more time falling off of them than actually doing any riding as a kid. In fact, I think I had thrown in the towel for good on the third or fourth try, blushing furiously and trying to ignore Hollis' laughter.

This time I was determined to succeed. Finally, I found the tiny little power button between one of the jets. Unlike a gravicycle, a hoverboard would only fly ten to twenty feet above the ground so hopefully I wouldn't hurt myself too badly if I did fall off. The board emitted an almost indiscernible hum as I pressed the button and let it drop to the ground, where it hovered one foot above the hard-packed Earth.

"Here goes nothing," I muttered and stepped on. Almost immediately it listed to one side and I bent my knees like I was surfing. I swore and gritted my teeth, talking to myself. "Ana, you can do this."

I focused on my spine, imagining a beam of light flowing from Anansanna overhead, through my head, down my spine, through my feet and down to the earth. Tethering me to the board. My shoes gripped the surface nicely. Maybe this wouldn't be so bad. Now that I was older, perhaps it'd be easier this time around. Slowly, I leaned forward a bit, putting my weight on to my toes, urging the board forward.

The damned thing practically shot out from under me and I had to bend my knees sharply as I tried to stay on. It was true, though, it did seem a little easier than it had been so many years ago. Perhaps it was the years of martial arts practice or maybe hiking all summer had given me more muscles and better balance but after traveling a few hundred feet along the road I was confident in my ability to stay on. As long as I didn't take any corners too quickly or change direction, like, ever, I thought I'd be okay.

Feeling more confident I hopped slightly in place, encouraging the board to go higher. Ten feet above the ground. Twenty. I was careful to give the city a wide berth as I headed towards to mountains of Niflhelf, worried that my red hair would act as a beacon to anyone that might recognize me. Honestly, the red light of the sun seemed to make it even more vibrant than ever. In Aeden, the fae were a varied people, with skin and hair colors ranging from every hue you could imagine on earth, and even some maybe you couldn't. Not everyone here was beautiful, but it was a rare sight to see a truly unattractive fae. Virtually all fae were tall, trim and athletic.

And then, there was me: short, curvy, red-haired, bright green eyes. Genetically, I seemed to owe more to my British Isles heritage than to the Fae. Here in Aeden, I stuck out, no matter how you looked at me. At least, that was how I had felt most of my life among my perfect family and friends. I'd always felt flawed. This summer, I'd started to feel better about myself. Stronger. More comfortable in my own body. Even before my powers had awakened, I'd started to feel like maybe I really was on equal footing with the rest of my peers. Now, I didn't like to think of my favorite physical trait as a weakness, but in this instance when I was trying to hide and escape there wasn't any other way to look at it. My red hair needed to stay out of sight and I didn't have a hat or a handkerchief to hide it under. I had to fly and fly fast, and pray no one saw me.

Khai could wake up at any moment. I wasn't the fastest runner and I certainly wasn't the best hoverboarder. I could only do my best, though I worried that it might not be enough. I shook that thought out of my head. It wouldn't help anything to think that way. I had to assume that I would make it.

On a gravicycle the flight from Valhalla to the Niflhelf portal entrance usually took one to two hours. On the hoverboard it would take at least twice that, probably more. I thought about heading towards one of the other portals, one that they wouldn't expect me to use, but I knew those were even further away. Plus, David had been taken in Montreal, not Arizona or Ireland where the next-closest portals let out, so Niflhelf it was.

After an hour, my legs were sore, the muscles twitching, letting me know that they wanted to move out of the stance I'd been holding. I tried to alleviate the boredom and fatigue by rocking from side to side, practicing my turns, but it wasn't enough. I simply wasn't used to this kind of exercise. My legs didn't have the muscles a hoverboard demanded. Sure, I'd walked miles and miles every day on the Long Trail in Vermont, but this was completely different. This was like asking somebody to squat in horse stance and hold it for an hour with no martial arts training. It just didn't quite seem possible.

Too bad I had no other choice. Terrified, I rode the board at breakneck speed, pushing it to its top speed, the countryside passing below in a blur. Looking down scared me even more, so I focused on the mountains that had become visible in the distance, trying to think of nothing but my goal.

After another hour, I'd reached the hills around the high mountains of Niflhelf. I couldn't feel my feet. The muscles in my knee had locked. My thighs were on fire. I was scared if I stopped I might not be able to start again, but I had to rest. I couldn't put it off a moment longer.

I tried descending and found that I had a hard time moving; unlocking my knees was almost impossible, but it had to be done because the only way to lower the hoverboard was to crouch, lowering my center of gravity.

Frustrated at my legs' lack of flexibility, I punched my thighs, willing my knees to bend. Suddenly, one popped and then the other. I almost fell off the board, catching myself just at the last moment, squatting atop the disc, clutching its sides with a white-knuckled grip. The board responded, dropping quickly towards the ground. My legs were shaking so much, I couldn't move and I decided to not bother trying. Instead, I let go, allowing myself to roll off the board onto the thick grass below.

Oh, thank heaven, it was Cala grass. Though often harvested for its nutritional properties, Cala grass was also used throughout Aeden in place of carpeting due to its ability to heal and energize fae cells through live-touch. For this reason, fae were almost always barefoot indoors. Legend had it that Cala was to thank for our survival across during the long journey across the stars. It seemed to enjoy a special bond with Anansanna, and so far efforts to grow it above below, in Midgard, had been fruitless.

Splaying my arms and legs out at my sides, I reveled in the sensation of life-giving energy flowing into me through every pore. Sighing, both in pain and relief, I closed my eyes.

It felt so good to allow my legs to do whatever they wanted. I hadn't even noticed but my body was covered with sweat from the dual exertion of maneuvering and staying balanced. Now, releasing that connection, my muscles were trembling. I didn't do anything to stop them, knowing that the Cala would heal me.

Twenty minutes to rest and recharge that was all I needed.

Just twenty minutes.

After the shaking had subsided, I opened my eyes and spotted some nearby bushes heavy with clusters of deep turquoise-colored berries. Crawling over to their drooping boughs, I picked several bunches, hungrily popping berry after berry into my mouth. The juicy fruits were hydrating and delicious, all at once. Surely, this meant that the gods were smiling upon my plan. I smiled at the boon and focused on eating my fill.

When I'd finished, I lifted my legs in the air, propping my hips with my hands and began cycling my legs, giving them the full range of motion they'd been crying for. After a few minutes of exercise, the pressure to keep moving weighed on me.

My healing powers had never worked well on my own body, but I decided to give it a shot, placing my hands on my chest and abdomen for a body scan.

Tired? Yes.

Overworked? You betcha.

What my body needed more than anything was rest, but that was something I couldn't give it. I focused on the most positive feelings I could: my deep love for my family; my hopes that David was okay. I tried activating my healing power, sending waves of wellness through my legs, focusing on my kneecaps and the surrounding muscles. There was a slight tingling but I could tell that it wasn't really working.

Self-healing was so much more difficult than healing someone else. Airmed said it was a question of learning how to use the energy around you instead of your own, but it wasn't something we'd practiced yet. I'd been so focused on helping David, I hadn't thought about how important it might be that I learn to help myself first. Somehow, I knew this would not be the most difficult day I'd be facing in the coming days as I tried to find David. Frustrated and feeling stupid, I sagged forward, stretching to reach my toes. If I couldn't heal myself, at least I could stretch my sore muscles.

Unbidden, my dreams came back to me. David's kiss. The pasty-faced man's laughter. Shivers of discomfort flew along my spine just remembering how he'd glammed himself, pretending to be David and then Khai. At the thought of Khai, a new sense of urgency overtook me. He must have woken up by now, discovered I was missing. I knew he wouldn't give up until he found me, that his search would be relentless. Like he'd said, we were family.

He'd promised my parents he'd look after me. There was no way he was going to just let me go running after David without a fight.

I clambered to my knees, getting back to the board and picking up the weighty apparatus. The rest of my journey wasn't going to be any easier, but I'd made progress. That was what I needed to focus on.

"Just keep going," I whispered to myself, holding the board in my hands against my chest like a shield. I took a deep breath, stared up at the brilliant vermillion sun and focused on pulling its energy down into my body. I visualized the sparkles flowing down my spine, through my shins, into the ground below me. "Center."

I forced all thoughts of David, Khai and the dream warper from my mind. Now was not the time to worry about what was chasing me. I needed to stay focused on my goal. My father had always been fond of quoting Sun Tzu during training, and now I remembered the line "If you know heaven and earth, you may make your victory complete." I'd always figured he liked it because he was an earth fae, but now, anchoring myself between Anansanna and the earth, I thought maybe Sun Tzu had been talking about something else. True balance was real power. Worrying about getting caught would only be a waste of mental energy. I needed to focus on strategy, and right now my best bet was to keep moving.

With renewed strength and resolve, I dropped the hoverboard to the ground, stepped on and kept my weight in my toes as I executed a few slight hops. The board began moving forward, climbing steadily into the air, matching the incline of the Niflhelf Mountain Range as it grew.

Chapter 7

I rode the hoverboard high over hillsides, tracing the trajectories of cliffs and rubble-strewn mountains, ever rising towards the entrance to the portal that would take me to Midgard. Also often called "above-below" by the residents of Aeden, the surface of our planet had been ruled for millennia by humans, but no more. Now the fae denizens of "hollow earth" and the humans outside mingled freely and happily, sharing technology and traditions.

When I finally flew into the dark tunnel, I could scarcely believe I had made it so far without being caught. The tunnel was dark, crystals embedded in the walls glowing green and purple. On a gravicycle, most people would need to use headlights to navigate the many twists and turns at high-speed, although my parents and brother rarely did since as earth fae they could see in the dark. All my life, I had traveled the tunnels in darkness, riding behind my mom or dad, the luminescent stones speeding by in a blur like I was on some crazy roller coaster ride.

Now, though, I was on the hoverboard. No torch or headlights to guide my way – and I found I didn't need them. I could see everything. Remaining tethered to Anansanna's energy through my spine, I could see beyond light and dark, beyond color. The crystals on the walls and ceiling of the tunnel weren't purple and green as I'd always believed. They were emitting colors that I'd never seen before, their lights pulsing shining back and forth to each other as if they were tapping out some sort of luminescent Morse code. It was gorgeous, another amazing sight to add to my ever-growing list of things that nobody had ever hinted I might experience some day.

My family hadn't prepared me for being a water fae. No one had ever spoken to me about what it was like. Fae didn't usually go around talking about their powers or abilities – one's powers were a private thing, not something to boast about or compare notes on. So even though I'd grown up knowing water fae, no one had mentioned the emotional feedback they got from people or talked about what it felt like to get this sort of sensory overload from the entire world. As a group, water fae probably wouldn't have talked about it even if it wasn't taboo. How could you expect anyone to understand what it was like to be so open, so sensitive? I wished I had somebody to talk to about it all now, someone who would understand. Someone other than Airmed, a person who had no interest in keeping me prisoner.

An idea started to form in my head for where I could go next, assuming I reached the surface. I found it amazing that I hadn't run into any guards yet. Did everyone really think that I was so inept? They hadn't even bothered to post people at the entrance to the portal. I should have been ecstatic to be underestimated, after all, it meant I could get away more easily, but I found it infuriating. I would show them. I'd find David and save him myself. That ought to give everyone a new respect for my capabilities.

I rode through the tunnels for miles, zooming along as fast as the hoverboard could travel. Finally, the tunnel opened up, revealing a vast cavern dimly lit with motion-sensing lights. Lined up against the walls, gravicycles sat ripe for the taking. I slowed down, considering.

Did I dare take one, leaving the hoverboard here? The Light Guard kept count of all the gravicycles coming in and out of Valhalla. I didn't know if the vehicles had tracker units on them or not – using one might tip my hand, revealing the way I'd come. I trailed my hand along one of the golden flying machines, built to resemble vintage skimobiles while outpacing them in every way. The machines were beautiful, sleek and almost as fun to ride as one of the Fleet. Staying on the board was probably the safest option. Then again, taking one could significantly widen the gap between me and pursuers. My legs trembled in agreement, speaking up for themselves. Every muscle, every fiber was screaming at me, letting me know that this was not up for debate. Even if I was capable of riding another half hour through the tunnel to the surface, there was no way that I would be able to walk out of the woods or even drive a car after the distance I'd come. My legs were on the point of collapse.

Casting aside any doubts or concerns I might have, I slid the hoverboard under a cycle along the far side of the cavern and hoped that no one would see it for a long time. Climbing on and pressing the ignition key with a small flick of my wrist, I was off, hurtling towards the surface. At one point, I passed through the place where the barrier used to stand, a force field of Druid magic and earth power that had once kept humans and Dark fae from discovering the faerie realms below. Now, of course, the barrier was down, a part of our past that was no longer needed, an ancient construct consigned to history and legend. Humans and fae were free to come and go from Aeden as they pleased – at least, most of us were.

The upward climb was so much faster than the hoverboard, and such a relief. My legs felt like jelly against the machine, boneless and weak. I flipped a switch on the dash, turning on the cycle's headlights, and released my connection to Anansanna, relaxing entirely.

All of a sudden, a voice crackled over the comm-unit in front of me.

"Anansanna Alvarsson, do you hear me?" Dorian Claffsson's voice was loud and grumpy, even through the comm-link. "If you can hear me, you should know your father wants you to turn around right now. Come back to Valhalla immediately."

I was tempted to shoot off a rude response but that would only reveal my whereabouts. They didn't know that I had grabbed a cycle. They didn't know where I was. They were probably broadcasting over every comm-unit in Valhalla, maybe even in Aeden. They might have been doing it for hours, or this could be the first time. I had no way of knowing. Either way, I had no intention of turning back. I was on a mission and a stern reprimand from the Light Commander was not going to deter me from my goal. I started to turn the comm-link off when a second voice crackled over the speakers.

"Ana, please, come back. We can talk about this. We'll figure something out. Just don't-"

My hand twitched, part of me wanting to listen to Khai, to turn around. Annoyed, I turned the unit off.

They still had no idea where I was. No one could imagine little Ana had really made it this far. For the first time since I'd left, I allowed myself to really smile. I whooped, ecstatic to be free.

"I'm coming, David," I vowed under my breath. "I just hope I'm not too late."

It wasn't much farther to the surface, just a couple minutes on the cycle and then I was bursting out into the light of day, the cool sunlight strange against my eyes. For a moment, I hovered in the air, idling, wondering if I dared borrow a less conspicuous vehicle from the nearby garage. Standing next to a new log cabin among the firs, the massive building could have been an air hangar. Both buildings had been refurbished recently, a nod to the increased traffic of both fae and humans between Aeden and Midgard. Since the fae had come out of hiding thirty years ago, there was no reason to hide the portal, or our coming and going. Many portals in other regions had evolved into small villages, waystations between Aeden and Midgard. Here, deep in the wild north of Canada, there were fewer travelers so things were evolving more slowly. The tiny one-room cabin masquerading as a hunter's lodge was gone, and the rough dirt trail through private land had been smoothed and paved to make it easier for visitors to reach the portal.

When I'd passed through a few weeks ago, Khai had parked our car between a small solar EV8 all-terrain vehicle and a trio of silver hover-cycles. There had been an old Chevord pickup, two older EV6s, and a dirt-bike covered with, what else, dirt. I knew from experience that most people left their keys in the vehicles, just in case someone else needed a ride. I could take whatever I wanted and no one would be too put out about it. I also knew that nothing was faster than a gravicycle.

"Screw it," I muttered, and made my decision. I pointed the gravicycle skyward and barreled through a break in the trees overhead. "Montreal, here I come."

Chapter 8

Rather than engaging the bike's navigation system, I followed the roads heading southeast towards the city. I'd driven this way enough times to know the route.

About halfway to Montreal, I started wishing I had taken one of the cars in the garage. The sun was out, but the air was crisp and cool, the smell of autumn on the wind. Below me, many of the trees had already begun to change color, donning vibrant hues of vermillion and gold to replace their usual summer greens. I'd forgotten how quickly the seasons changed this far north. Goosebumps along my arms reminded me I'd be needing warmer clothes, something to replace the loose linen shorts and fitted halter top I'd put on this morning.

By the time I spotted the city suburbs in the distance, my skin had gone numb. Soon, the sun would be setting and I really needed to find some shelter and get warmed up. I knew that Jules had found an apartment for us near McGill, but I didn't know where. Bringing my cycle down to land on top of the school's largest library, I hoped someone in the building would be able to help me out. When I'd interviewed at the school, we'd started at the Welcome Center at the McLennan. Surely, a place designed to help new students feel at ease would be willing to help a girl find her friend.

Peering over the edge of the roof, I could see people walking between buildings and relaxing on the huge lawns. A couple of the kids below were playing openly with their powers, tossing balls of fire back and forth to each other. It was a bit warmer here in the city, the brick building radiating heat, but I was still chilled. At least my feet were not bare, since I'd borrowed Airmed's woven moccasins to collect acorns in the forest. I walked over to the door that would lead downstairs and pulled. Of course, it was locked. Base jumping had become a huge craze in the last few years at colleges, and the university wouldn't want to be responsible for kids leaping off school property. Frustrated, I put my hands out in front of me and threw a pulse of energy at the door, intending to knock the bolt loose. The steel door blasted backwards, right off its hinges.

Oops. Someone would need to fix that. I bit my lip and tried to lift the door to at least give it the appearance of being closed, but it was too heavy for my small frame to budge. Not waiting around to get caught at the scene of the crime, I ran down the steps as fast as I could. The warmth of the building welcomed me. Finally, I was on the ground floor at the Welcome Center. They had revamped the place since the last time I was here, painted the walls in a rich gold paint against which a scarlet and white school crest gleamed, carved from wood. An actual banner draped across the wall declaring the school motto: "Grandescunt Aucta Labore" – by work, all things increase and grow.

"How can I help you today, miss," an older woman asked, taking in my appearance. "You girls these days. You really should put on more clothes."

"I know, believe me. I didn't realize that it would be so cold today."

"Cold? This is the warmest day we've had in over a week." She looked at me oddly.

"Right, yeah. Actually, I just flew in from Florida and I'm supposed to be meeting my friend. She was going to show me around the college this week but I've totally forgotten where she's living. Some guys told me to check in here, that you'd be able to help me?" I tried to say this as cluelessly as possible, hoping she'd buy the act.

The woman rolled her eyes, clearly not thinking I was McGill material, but she seemed to buy my story.

"Alright, well we can't have you wandering around the campus freezing to death." She called up her holo-screen and opened the student directory. "What's your friend's name?"

"Jules Harrison."

"J-e-w-e-l-s?"

"No, J-u-l-e-s."

"Okay, great, here she is. Your friend is living off campus, but not too far away, just a few blocks north of here." She rattled off directions along with the address and I thanked her.

"It's kind of a long way to walk. How are you going to get there with all your bags? Do you have money for taxi?" She leaned over the counter and saw that I didn't have any. I blushed.

"Oh, my bags... I left them outside in the hall by the door."

"This is a big city, you can't go around leaving your bags wherever you feel like it. Things do still go missing from time to time, you know."

"I know, I know. My dad told me," I said, scrambling to stay in character. "I just figured I shouldn't clutter up your office here."

"Kids these days," she muttered under her breath. "Look, even if the crime rates are down and almost non-existent, you should still keep a closer eye on your stuff. This isn't some small town in Florida where everybody knows everybody else, you know? This is real city. Better safe than sorry."

"I know," I repeated. "I really am sorry. I won't leave them anywhere again. Don't worry, I'll be okay."

"Okay," she said, looking at me doubtfully. "You know, I'm getting off in a few minutes, I could give you a ride-"

"No, that's okay. Please, don't worry."

"Alright. You know, I didn't catch your name. What is it?"

"It's An- Andrea. Andrea Ward," I fumbled, using my father's last name.

"Okay, Andrea Ward. Any relation to Hollis Ward?"

"Nope, never heard of him. Sorry." I started backing out of the office, cursing my stupidity inside. It was stupid to use his name. I should have picked something completely random like Frasier or Grasshopper.

"Oh, too bad. He's such a nice young man. He takes good care of us here, always offering to help out when we're doing events. He hosts prospective students all the time."

"Ah. Well, you know the name Ward, it does mean we take care of people. Must run in the genes." I smiled nervously, my hand on the doorknob behind me, ready to bolt.

She laughed. "Right. Although, my last name is Cantor and I can't sing a note."

"Genes, you never know what you're going to get, do you?"

"I guess not. Well, have a nice day, Andrea."

"Thanks, you too, Ms. Cantor." I slipped out the door and stood in the hallway for a moment, feeling terrible.

I couldn't help having some guilt about lying to this woman. I mean, she knew my brother. Pretty soon, if things went well, I'd be going to school here, too. What if she remembered me and knew that I lied?

I forced myself to remember David. This was for him – everything I was doing was to help him. Don Quixote had said that all was fair in love and war – well this was both, right?

I took a moment to memorize my route on a campus map outside the office and then I hustled out the front doors and took off, sprinting towards Jules' apartment building. I could only hope she'd be home when I got there. The pavement felt like hammers on the bottom of my feet as I ran, the thin leather soles of my moccasins doing nothing to protect me from the hard surface below. At least the run was getting my blood flowing. The short time I'd spent on the gravicycle had done wonders for my legs, but they were still tired. As I ran, I attempted to connect to Anansanna again, to collect some of her juicy energy flow but it was much harder up here on the surface.

As fast as I was running, I felt like I standing in quicksand and sinking fast.

Then it hit me. Of course I felt that way. I was trying to connect to Anansanna as if she was above me, when the red sun was actually deep below the ground below my feet. Instead of trying to connect to it the way that Khai had showed me, I began to imagine that I was drawing her energy up through my feet as I ran. Each time I raised my leg, I pulled the energy into me, my legs like super-straws. The flow was muted, but I could feel it. Red sparkles traveled up my legs, enlivening my hips, setting my torso on fire. When it reached my arms my chest expanded and I started to pump my arms faster, speeding down the sidewalk, apologizing as I darted between people.

Finally, I found Jules' place, a really modern building of gleaming chrome and glass. Not what I would have picked, but then, I wasn't here to help her look around. I was just glad she'd found a place near school. The front door had been propped open so I was able to just walk right inside. I checked the mail slots, confirming that Jules' name was on there – apartment 3C, just like Ms. Cantor had said. I was just about to head upstairs when a guy walked in carrying a large box of pizza.

"You apartment 2B?" he asked. I looked at the large recycled container in his hands and saw that the box for mushrooms had been marked with an "x".

"Is that a mushroom pizza?" It smelled amazing.

"You got it." He handed me the pizza and smiled.

"Um, actually, I just came in from a walk, my roommate ordered the pizza. Why don't you take it up?" I said, trying to hand it back. "I don't have any money on me."

"Nah, you're good, it's already paid for, tip and everything." Before I could say another word, the guy was out the door and out of sight.

Now I knew why the door had been propped open – probably by the person who was waiting for their dinner up on the second floor. I started up the stairs, planning on delivering it myself, but by the time I'd hit the second floor my mouth was watering from the steam emanating from the box. My foot hovered on the landing, and then I was walking past, quickly and quietly up to the third floor. I stopped in front of Jules' place, pulled out a slice of pizza and started eating even as I listened at the door. I couldn't hear any noise from inside or sense any auras, so I didn't think she was home. Still, I knocked on the door a few times and paused before sliding down to wait with my back to the door. At least I had a pizza to keep me company while I sat.

I'd already eaten three slices by the time I heard anyone moving in the halls downstairs. A door slammed below and a woman said something about being on the case, then I heard footsteps stomping up and down the hall below me. The person headed down the stairs to the ground floor, and then there were more footsteps going coming back up to the second floor, passing the second floor, and heading my way. Someone was looking for something, and I had a feeling that something might be what I'd been chomping on for the last twenty minutes.

"Fee fie foe fum, I smell pizza. Dum dum dum dum, dum dum dum dum," a girl's voice sang Beethoven's Fifth quietly. A dark head of hair poked into the hallway and charcoal eyes lighted on me. "Hey, you. Whose pizza is that there?"

"What? What do you mean; what pizza?" I could have smacked myself for how stupid I sounded. What pizza, really? What was I thinking?

"Um, the box sitting right next to you?"

"Oh, right, yeah, my friend ordered it for me. I'm just waiting to meet her."

"Really," the girl drawled, coming to stand over me. "'Cuz I'm pretty sure that's my pizza that I ordered over an hour ago. I called to see where it was, and do you know what they said?"

I swallowed. "No, what did they say?"

"They said that it had been delivered to a girl who lives with me. Funny thing is though, my roommate's a guy. So I'm guessing that somebody was you?"

Caught, I blushed and started babbling. "I'm sorry. It's been a really long day and I haven't eaten since breakfast and I'm waiting for my friend but she's not here and-"

"Whatever," she said, leaning down and grabbing the box off the floor. "You better come with me."

"Are you going to turn me in? I swear I really am waiting for my friend Jules. She'll pay back you when she gets here.

The girl slanted her eyes, examining me, and then noticed at the door I was sitting in front. "You're friends with Jules? How do you know her?"

"I'm her best friend from home."

"Oh, yeah? And where is that?"

"Falls Depot, Vermont."

"Ding-ding-ding! You win a prize, you are the lucky winner! You do know Jules." The girl's entire demeanor had changed, warming up in an instant. "Look, she's not going to be back until really late tonight, her team had a meet over in Quebec City. You should come and hang out with us until she gets back, she'd kill me if she knew I left one of her friends just waiting in the hallway in some flimsy shorts and t-shirt. Gods, girl don't you know how to dress for a Canadian autumn?"

I laughed uneasily. "Yeah, I know, stupid, right? Like I said, it's been a day... I'll be okay waiting here, don't worry about me."

"Please, I can't leave you waiting here in the hallway. Somebody might trip over you. You're a safety hazard. Come on, up you go." She reached out with one hand to help me up.

"Okay. I don't suppose you have hot chocolate in your apartment, do you?"

She laughed, a deep, rich sound. "Of course, I have hot chocolate. What kind of girl do you take me for? Come on, let's get you warmed up." She opened the box as we started walking down the hall. "Damn, girl! Three slices?"

"Sorry," I said, flushing.

"Okay, don't worry. I'm surprised someone as small as you can pack away so much food. I'll just have to start eating my share right now because the minute my roommate gets his hands on this, it's game over for me. I'm usually lucky if I can even get two slices out of a pie before he inhales the whole damn thing."

"Seriously? Who do you room with, a yeti?"

"I wish. At least a yeti wouldn't leave his clothes all over the place. But no, you'll see, my roomie's great, actually."

Chapter 9

I followed the girl into her apartment. She hadn't been kidding about her roommate. The place looked like it had been tossed by burglars. A coatrack by the door was mostly empty, boasting only a couple jackets and a pair of swim shorts, while sweatshirts and towels lay strewn about on the floor below, looking forlorn. Sneakers were piled up in a corner beside a couple pairs of ballet flats. It seemed like far too much debris to have come from just one lone male.

"How many roommates did you say you have?" I asked as I walked past her into the living room.

"Just one," she grumbled through a mouth full of crust, closing the door behind me.

"Reenah, is that you?" A voice was muffled, coming from another room. "Did you find it?"

"Yep, got it."

"Great!" The male voice got louder as a door opened, steam billowing out around a pale, half-naked body. Reenah's roommate stepped into the living room, toweling off a head of fine blonde hair. He looked at Reenah, smiling. "I'm starved." His eyes met mine over her shoulder and widened. "Ana?"

"Gawen?" I asked, surprised. I'd met Gawen the last time I'd been in Montreal, that first night we'd gone out clubbing after completing the Long Trail. We'd been so happy: Jules, David and I. We'd hit all my favorite spots, starting the evening slow listening to Irish ballads at Clancy's and ending hard with tribal beats at Zora's. Zora's had always been a fae hotspot, even before the flare. Most of the employees were fae and it always had the best music. But when I'd seen the crowd dancing in the dark, their energy soaring as they danced, I'd been stunned. The pumped up fae auras had become an auroral mingling, the best light show I'd ever seen. Gawen had picked me out of the crowd and explained what I was experiencing. As a fellow water fae, he'd been able to see my own energy and tell what I was going through. Right away, he'd come over and offered to help me brush up on my new powers. To be honest, he'd hit on me a bit, but once he had seen that I was with David he'd backed off.

"What are you doing here," Gawen asked, pulling his sweatpants up a bit higher on his waist.

"You know her?" Reenah said surprised.

"Yeah, I met her over the summer."

"She's supposed to be Jules' roommate, you know, the new girl up on the third floor?"

"Oh, right." Gawen looked at me, eyes narrowed. "Aren't you supposed to be down in Aeden? Jules said you were doing some sort of special study project down there."

I choked back a cynical laugh. Jules had really sugar-coated it for her new friends. "Yeah, well, I'm here now. Just for a visit," I quickly clarified. "I'm not sure when I'll be starting at school."

"Get this, she's the one who stole our pizza," Reenah said. "So, Ana, is it?"

"Yeah, Ana Alvarsson."

"Nice to meet you," Reenah said, quirking one pierced eyebrow as she shook my hand. "I'm Reenah Shin."

"And I don't believe I ever properly introduced myself. Last name's Black." Gawen shook my hand. "So, you're the pizza thief, eh?"

"Sorry. The delivery guy came in right after me and just kind of handed it to me. I was really hungry." I shrugged, chewing my lip. "I was planning on paying you back, you know, eventually."

"Sure you were," Reenah said, laughing. "Anyways, here you go, Gawen."

Gawen opened the box. "But it's already half gone!"

"Don't look at me," Reenah said. "I just ate a piece on the way down. Blame Ana."

"Sorry," I apologized again. Gawen looked at me, taking in my tangled hair and bare feet.

"You look like you had a rough journey," he said.

"I don't know what you mean," I said, batting my eyelashes innocently.

"Hasn't anyone told you that it's useless lying to a water fae?" He smiled back at me, but his silver eyes held disappointment.

"Right, well, it's kind of a long story."

"Perfect, my favorite kind," he quipped.

"Mine, too," said Reenah. "Why don't you guys sit on the couch while I go make that hot chocolate I promised you?"

"Maybe you can scrounge up some sweats for this girl, too, while you're at it."

"Just so long as they're not his," I called as I pushed some junk off the couch.

Reenah laughed. "No way, never his."

"Hey," he said, sounding offended. "What do you mean? My clothes are clean." Reenah and I looked at each other and burst out laughing. What?"

"Maybe you can explain to him what closets are for," Reenah said as disappeared into her room shaking her head.

"I know what closets are for," Gawen muttered as he bit off a huge piece of pizza.

"You sure? Prove it, start using yours," I said.

"I do. It just takes me awhile to get things organized, that's all. I'm a very busy person. I'm involved in a lot of activities here at school."

"Really like what? I asked.

"Well, classes, obviously. And I'm on the water polo team."

"That would explain the pile of towels by the door. But you know, they dry out a lot better if you hang them up."

"Oh gods, you sound like my mom."

"Sorry," I laughed, taking another slice of pizza. "She sounds like a wise woman."

Gawen stared at me. "Where do you put it all? You can't possibly still be hungry."

"I may look little, but I'm big on the inside," I quipped.

Reenah came back into the room and threw a track suit at me, striped fleecy pants with a matching zip-up jacket. "Here, put these on. They'll fit right over what you're wearing."

"Oh, thanks." I put the pieces on, letting the long pants hang over my feet for extra warmth. "These are great."

"Sorry they are so long. I should have given you capris, I guess." She handed me some socks and went into the kitchen.

"No, they're perfect, really." Like most fae, Reenah was tall and lithe, blessed with a ballet dancer's body. I pulled on the socks and then settled back into the couch, polishing off my fourth slice while Reenah filled up a pot of water to boil for the hot chocolate.

"Alright." She came back and sat next to me. "Spill. What's going on with you?"

I pursed my lips, thinking. I didn't know these people at all. I probably shouldn't tell them anything but I needed to talk to somebody and Jules wasn't home. Maybe they could help.

"What makes you think anything is going on?"

"Oh, please. Don't test me."

"You're fae, right?" I asked her.

"Yeah, air."

"Are you guys, like, together?"

Gawen and Reenah looked at each other and started laughing. "Ew, gods, no," Reenah said when she could breathe again.

"Our moms were best friends growing up," Gawen began.

Reenah nodded, picking up where he left off. "But my parents died when I was really young in a freak diving accident. Their bodies were never recovered. Gawen's parents took me in, raised us like brother and sister."

"Oh, wow. I'm sorry about your parents." Losing David was tearing me up inside. I couldn't begin to imagine losing my mom or dad.

"Yeah, me too. It's been almost ten years now. Hard to believe that they're really gone sometimes, you know? We're supposed to live such long lives. I don't know. I guess they thought they were immortal or something and weren't. The Coast Guard found their boat, but they never recovered the bodies. They must have run into some sharks or something. We'll never really know what happened."

Gawen patted her hand looking sad enough for the both of them. "She cried for three months, don't let her fool you."

I could see her energy just as well as he could and the sadness muddying her aura was thick. She did a good job hiding it now. If you weren't a water fae you would never know how much she still hurt on the inside.

"So anyways," she said overly brightly, "tell us what's going on with you. I don't need a pity party but I have a feeling maybe you do." Reenah pierced me with a glance. She might not be a water fae, but she obviously had her own gift of intuition.

"Gawen, do you remember that guy I was with when we met at the club?" I asked, deciding to start there.

"The human?" he asked, shoving some pizza crust into his mouth.

"Well, it turns out he's not really human, not entirely."

"What do you mean? There's no way he's part fae."

"He's not, not even remotely. He's starseed."

"He's what now?" Reenah said, confused.

"Starseed. His family is descended from off-world beings that interbred with humans thousands of years ago."

"Are you talking aliens?" Gawen demanded.

"Yep. Don't sound so surprised. It's not like it can't happen. I mean basically this whole planet was created by aliens: us."

"I guess... if you believe in that story." Gawen sounded skeptical.

"You guys don't believe the creation stories?"

"I guess I never really thought about it much," he said, shrugging.

"It's kind of hard to wrap your head around," Reenah said, agreeing with Gawen. Obviously, their parents hadn't personally climbed the World Tree and caused the flare, so I couldn't fault their preference for a rational world.

"I never thought about it much either, I guess, until I met David. I should start at the beginning. Has Jules told you anything about her summer?"

Chapter 10

"Sure, you guys spent a month hiking the Long Trail, right? We heard all about it – America's oldest long-distance trail, Vermont's greatest treasure, blah blah blah," Reenah droned.

"Exactly. Well, I didn't know I was a water fae until we were deep in the woods. I was kind of a late bloomer, my powers never activated when I had my Ascension, or at least if they did I didn't notice. My whole life, I expected to be an earth fae someday, like my family, so if there was anything going on before that I didn't notice. But when we went hiking my powers really came out. I even made it rain."

"Oh yeah, Jules talked about that," Gawen said, lighting up as he remembered. "She said you made it rain for a whole week."

"Well, I don't think I started the rain, but it seems the more upset I got about it, the more it rained. That's what we think happened anyways."

"Wow. That's really cool. I haven't been able to manipulate the weather at all. I can do some other cool things with water, though," he said.

"Really? You'll have to teach me. I still don't know much. Airmed's been concentrating on teaching me shielding techniques and how to control my emotions."

"Airmed, like The Airmed? The Ancient?" Gawen squawked. "That's who you've been studying with?"

"Yep."

"Again, wow. I'm so jealous right now."

"Well, just wait until you hear the rest of my story," I warned.

"Okay, we're listening." The tea kettle went off and Reenah got up to make the hot chocolate.

"So anyways, what happened was I kind of got in a fight with my friend Khai."

"A fire fae?" Gawen asked, a knowing grin on his face.

"Yeah, how'd you know?"

"Fire fae are always the easiest ones to fight with, especially for a water fae. We know just how to get on each other's nerves."

In the kitchen, Reenah laughed. "Ain't that the truth? You should have seen him last year with these guys-"

Gawen cut her off. "We can share war stories later. Right now it's Ana's turn."

I tried to rein in my smile, loving their easy banter. It had been so long since I'd been around people I wasn't mad at, I'd forgotten what a normal conversation felt like.

"So, I got in a fight with Khai over I don't even know what. I was really pissed and I ran off into the woods, no GPS or anything. By the time I noticed, I was already hopelessly lost, and I'd managed to call in a massive thunderstorm – not that I knew it had anything to do with me, of course."

"Of course," Gawen nodded enthusiastically, getting into my tale.

"Lightning started striking all over the place and all I could think of was that I needed to get to shelter or get back to camp, but I didn't know where camp was so I just kept running, looking for a place to hide. Thunderstorms are really dangerous when you're out in the woods. All those trees are like antennas."

"And you were basically acting like a lightning rod, since you were what drew the storm in the first place," Gawen supplied.

"Right, exactly. But I didn't know that yet so there I was running through the woods, totally terrified. I slid down a hill into the middle of a camp full of yurts. It was weird, of course, but I figured that it was some research group or some hippies or something. I saw everybody taking shelter in the yurts, and decided to do the same, heading for the closest one. I was expecting to find a bunch of cots or maybe more scientists huddled around their research, but instead there were cells."

"What do you mean, like jail cells?" Reenah asked, handing me a steaming mug of chocolatey goodness.

I inhaled the steam gratefully and nodded. "Exactly, like a prison, and there were people inside being held captive."

"Seriously? That's crazy!" she said.

"I know right? Even crazier was that I recognized one of the people in a cell, someone I had met on the trail just a few days earlier. We'd hung out and eaten dinner together, and he'd seemed like a really nice guy, so when I saw him there I just knew that he couldn't deserve to be locked up like that."

"Ah, your water senses were kicking in. You've got intuitive superpowers now, Ana, don't forget that," Gawen said seriously, tapping his forehead.

"Yeah, well this guy, he was good and I knew it. His cousin had gone missing hiking the same trail earlier in the season and he'd been tracing her footsteps, trying to pick up a clue to what had happened. It was David."

"Oh, wow. This is better than a mystery novel." Reenah snuggled up under a blanket, looking suitably freaked out.

"Everybody started clamoring for me to let them out, never mind the storm outside. They knew the people who had locked them up were deadlier than any electrical storm. We all ran out into the woods, scattering in different directions. I don't even know if everybody got away or if some of the people wound up caught, but David and I headed back the way I'd come. We ran a long time, and David explained what was going on at the camp. Eventually, Khai and my brother, Hollis, found us. Hollis is an earth fae so he was able to talk to the animals and find out which way I'd gone." I smiled and laughed, remembering what had happened next. "When they saw David trailing behind me, they both attacked David, assuming that I was running from some crazed rapist in the woods or something. I had to calm them both down before they'd listen to me, and decided not to tell them about the prison camp. I told them I had found David in the woods, and that we were just running from the rainstorm. Looking back now, I can see it was really stupid of me, but I'd been looking forward to that hiking trip my whole last year of school. I knew Hollis would call my dad and that would be the end of our trip."

I took a careful sip of cocoa, the scalding liquid's temperature just shy of tongue-burning. "It made David uncomfortable, but he felt like he owed me for saving him, so he stayed quiet. I think my family still hasn't forgiven me for that, for lying to them. It was stupid and immature, I know that now, but at the same time I can't help feeling glad that I did, because honestly what they did next just proved me right. They think a toddler could take better care of herself, I swear."

"Can we get to the part where you explain about the aliens? I'm so confused right now. Who took David hostage, the government?" Reenah demanded.

"Not the government. Warpers. The same people that took his cousin."

"What the hell is a warper?" Gawen asked, leaning forward and starting in on the last piece of pizza.

"Starseeds gone bad. From the very beginning, some starseeds haven't been able to handle their powers-"

"Starseeds have powers? Like us?" Reenah's eyes had gone wide.

"Sort of. There are five main powers, all what most people would call 'psychic,' I guess. Some can read minds, some astral travel and dreamwalk, some have telekinesis. The ones that tend to cause the most trouble are the guys who can make you see or do whatever they want, creating holograms or using mind control."

"Ew. Okay, so, not like us," said Reenah.

"Back in the day, I guess it caused some big wars, with the humans revolting. Eventually, a truce was called, but it involved the aliens who had birthed the starseeds leaving the planet. The starseeds have been policing themselves ever since. They have their own ruling body called the Gregors. Still, sometimes starseeds minds get twisted by their powers and that's when they're called warpers – because they ruin and warp everything around them."

"Heavy," Gawen sighed, patting his stomach as he laid back in his seat. "But I still don't get it. How can any of them go bad now? I mean, didn't the flare take care of all the drama?"

"Unfortunately, no. Their DNA is too different. Whatever it is that gives them their powers, it also makes them immune to the effects of Anansanna. So no enhanced healing. No long life spans. And no extra powers."

"Ah. That kind of sucks," Gawen said, stating the obvious.

"They certainly think so. At least, the warpers do. David thinks they are trying to level the playing field with their more recent experiments, maybe even find a way to take out the fae."

"Wow. So we have enemies we didn't even know existed. Someone needs to warn the Light Council," Reenah said.

"Don't worry. They know," I said, thinking of David. "Honestly, at this point I don't really even care about the warpers. I don't want to save the world, I just want to save David."

Reenah and Gawen looked at me, confused. "What do you mean?" she asked.

"I should finish the rest of the story, then it will all make more sense. That day at camp, we all agreed David could finish the trail with us. He wanted to get back to Montreal so he could warn the Gregors here what was going on, but of course we didn't tell the others that. One day Khai was being a jerk, making fun Jules and we all got in a huge fight."

"Oh, Jules told me all about that," Reenah exclaimed. "Khai made some kind of bet with you that Hollis would make her cry, right? She's still mad at Hollis for breaking her heart, you know. He stops by every few days, and she makes him talk to her from outside in the hallway."

"Good for her. He's an idiot if he thinks he can do better than Jules. And Khai... Well, I was so mad that he could even think about that stupid bet when Jules was hurting. He wanted to make David leave the group, he knew we were hiding something, I guess. We split up: Khai continuing on with Hollis; Jules, David and I on our own. Overall, it was a lot more peaceful that way, although we did run into another warper at one point on the trail, a grammer who pretended to have a gun. Luckily, I was able to take care of him with my own powers. By the time we arrived in Montreal, I knew two things for sure: the warpers were seriously bad news, and David and I were falling for each other."

"Wasn't he, like, way older than you?" Gawen asked.

"Not that much older, he's twenty-nine, just ten years. Age differences don't mean anything to fae, so who cares?" I asked testily.

"But if his DNA isn't shifting like other humans-" Reenah started.

"We'll take whatever time we can get, okay. It's not like we're getting married, geez." I rolled my eyes. "Focus, guys. Story, remember? Anyhow, the next day I brought David to the Gregor headquarters. I was planning on going to Aeden for a little while to train with Airmed before school, and was supposed to catch up with him when I got back. But that's not how it worked out."

"What happened?" Reenah asked, gazing at me over her mug, spellbound.

"He was taken. The warpers, they hit the whole compound. They took everyone. And we have no idea where David or any of the Montreal starseeds are. My family has been working with Airmed to keep me captive down in Valhalla. They're convinced I'll something stupid."

"Like go after David on your own?" Gawen drawled.

I blushed. "Something like that. I know, I don't have great track record right now. But I can't stand by meditating every day in a garden when my boyfriend is being tortured, or worse."

"Oh my gods, you're going after him. It's so romantic." Reenah clasped a pillow to her chest.

"Or stupid," Gawen said drily. "You realize you're blowing off an Ancient?"

"Airmed? She'll forgive me," I said with breezy confidence.

"How many people were at these headquarters, anyways?" Gawen asked, changing tack.

"I'm not sure. Somewhere between forty and ninety people, we think. My dad went to Boston to talk to the starseeds there, but the trail's gone cold." For a moment, I felt overwhelmed by hopelessness. "No one knows where they are, or what is going to happen to them. And it's all my fault."

"How could it be your fault?" Reenah demanded.

"I don't know." I wiped a stray tear from my cheek. "I mean, if I hadn't made David keep things a secret when we were on the Long Trail, if I'd told Hollis and my parents sooner, maybe all this could have been avoided. Maybe David wouldn't have been at headquarters that day. Maybe he would have been in Boston or somewhere else."

"Coulda, woulda, shoulda," Gawen said. "You can't change history. All you can do is move forward."

"Gawen's right," Reenah said. "You can't change history. I should know – that's been my mantra for the last ten years."

I looked at her, feeling like an idiot. "What I'm going through probably seems insignificant next to your loss. Gods, I'm sorry."

"Are you kidding? My parents, yeah, they died and it sucks, okay? But your boyfriend, he's still alive. If we can do something about it, I'm all for it. I don't believe in wallowing in the past or crying over things I can't change. At least, not too much. Believe me, I've shed a lot of tears. But it's important to look forward. A lot of people's lives are at stake, from what you're saying. My parents knew diving is dangerous. Accidents happen. Maybe they were eaten by some giant shark or maybe they got stuck in some underwater cave, hey, who knows? It doesn't matter, either way they're gone. But the people you're talking about, they were just trying to live their lives. What these warpers are doing sucks. Whatever we can do to help, I'm with you."

"But you don't even know me," I protested weakly.

"I don't need to know you. If Gawen and Jules are friends of yours then you're a friend of mine."

"I don't know what to say."

"You don't need to say anything. You need to plan. Lucky for you that's one of my favorite things," Gawen said with a grin, leaning forward with his arms on his knees.

Reenah laughed. "Seriously, planning really is his thing. You should see the elaborate pranks he pulls at home."

"I'm not sure if pulling a prank equates to going up against a league of warpers," I mused.

"Well, it will have to do. To hear you tell it, our own guards aren't following through, so we'll do it ourselves," Gawen vowed.

"But, you guys have classes. I can't ask you to help me. I just stopped here to see Jules so I could get some warm clothes, stock up on supplies and keep moving."

"So, what's your game plan?" Gawen demanded.

"I figured I'd go to Boston maybe, or head down near where their camp was. See if I could find anything there."

"Haven't your parents and the guards already done that?" Reenah asked.

"Yeah, but-"

"But nothing." Gawen's tone was firm. "Look, we've got your back. We're going to do this together, end of story. Right, Reenah?"

"Hells yeah. I'm doing an independent study this semester. I don't even have to actually be on campus. So far it's just been research, research, research, every day at the library. I can do that from anywhere, and my advisor is chill. It won't matter if I hand in my project a little late. But it will matter if something bad happens because you felt like you had to do this on your own." Reenah leaned over and put her hand on my shoulder. "Okay?"

"Okay," I said, blowing out a breath I hadn't even realized I'd been holding.

"Good. I'm going to send Jules a message, let her know you're here. I'm guessing you didn't do that yet?" She looked at me with her eyebrows raised.

"No. All I brought with me from Valhalla is the clothes on my back. I don't even have my chat device."

"That's not a problem. I just got a new one for my birthday, and haven't decommissioned my old one yet. You can have mine," she said, heading into her bedroom to get the chats and make the call.

I leaned back on the couch, feeling overwhelmed. Reenah didn't take long, jolting me out of my daydreams when she came back and tossed a small piece of flesh-colored plastic at me. The tiny communications piece was designed to rest in your ear, allowing you to talk with anyone, anywhere, anytime using voice commands. The new models even allowed you to call up a holo-screen, so you could vid-chat with friends.

"Thanks," I said, fumbling the catch and putting it in my left ear.

"Anytime." She smiled and picked up the empty pizza box and mugs, and gestured for Gawen to help her in the kitchen.

I imagined they probably had some things to discuss on their own, so I stayed on the couch. The luxurious weight of the carbs and cheesy goodness in my stomach combined with my exhaustion, begging me to sleep. I closed my eyelids, promising myself it would just be for a moment.

Chapter 11

It was the whisper of voices that woke me some hours later, the quiet susurration of his and hers tenors and altos. Stretching my arms above my head, I opened my eyes and looked around warily. I was still on the couch in the apartment, piles of towels and clothes on the floor nearby, books stacked up on the coffee table.

I got up, following the sound of the voices to a bedroom. Jules, Reenah and Gawen were all sitting together on a bed, heads bent close together as they talked in low voices.

"Jules!" I cried out happily, launching myself at her.

"Ana!" Jules jumped up, enveloping me in one of her Amazonian hugs. "It's so great to see you, wow!"

"We've been filling her in on what's going on," Reenah volunteered.

"I had no idea things were so bad," Jules said, detangling herself from my arms and looking down at me, clearly upset on my behalf.

"Yeah, well... I imagine that Khai and my family have been patting themselves on their backs, believing they're doing such a great thing keeping me safe, when the fact is all they've been doing is keeping me crazy."

Jules laughed without humor. "Hollis does kind of have a knack for making people crazy."

"Tell me about it," I agreed. "Although honestly, I don't even care about any of it anymore. Staying angry is just too exhausting. All I really care about is getting David safe."

"I hear that," she said. "Come here, let me show you what we have so far for a plan."

Gawen showed me a sheet of paper where he had started brainstorming. Some items were crossed out, while others had notes next to them like "too crazy?" and "dangerous, but maybe..."

"I know you said that Light Guards have already gone to the campsite in the woods and that they didn't find anything, and that they've been over the Gregor building here, too, but I can't help thinking that maybe they just aren't looking hard enough."

"Or maybe they're looking in the wrong place," Jules said. "Like, has anyone been to Baltimore to check out his cousin's old place?"

"David said that was a dead end, the police there never found anything."

"Yeah, but they weren't really looking, were they? I mean, they thought Clarise and her boyfriend got lost on the trail. They didn't know that Tom was a warper, or that he lured her into becoming one of them on the hike. Which means they might have missed something," Jules pointed out.

"You're right," I exclaimed, starting to feel hopeful.

"Yeah, so Baltimore might have some leads. Also Boston – you said that was where your dad went next to talk to the Gregors." Gawen looked at me for confirmation.

"Mmm. But it was a dead end. The starseeds have no leads, either."

"So you were told. But we were thinking-" Gawen looked at Jules and Reenah, pausing.

"Tell her," Jules said.

"Well," Gawen rushed on. "We were thinking that maybe your family hasn't been telling you the truth."

"What do you mean?" I asked, straightening up.

"Think about it," Reenah said, looking apologetic. "Up till now, their top priority seems to have been keeping you safe. What if they did find a lead and they just haven't told you about it because they think it's too dangerous or too scary for you to know about?"

My stomach lurched. The idea was horrifying and yet part of me knew instantly that that's exactly what had happened. "Oh my gods! I never even thought of that. I have to call my dad."

"No!" They all yelled at once.

"You cannot call your dad. You can't call anyone in your family. Don't even think about it, unless you want a one-way ticket straight back to Aeden," Gawen warned.

"Geez, okay," I said, feeling cowed.

"Look, we're in this together, remember?" Gawen said more softly. "We're not going to let you do anything stupid. Or if we do, we'll all do it together. As a group."

"Wow, that makes me feel so much better. Stupid as a group." My voice held a healthy dose of snark.

"Yeah, well, it's better than stupid by yourself," Jules said, bumping shoulders with me.

I answered her grin with one of my own. "Okay, so how do we find out what they know?" The thought of sneaking around my brother's apartment, or worse, my dad's office, made me feel queasy.

"I think we need to go back to the beginning, check out the Gregor headquarters," Gawen said. "Together, two water fae can pick up a huge amount of information – I wouldn't be surprised if we discover more than the Guards did."

"What do you mean?"

"As water fae, we can pick up the emotions people have left behind. Working together, we can actually experience the history of a place, at least, the really emotional times. I'm guessing that warpers hijacking a bunch of starseeds will qualify as one of those situations, something strong enough to leave an imprint for us to track."

"How is that even possible? Besides, if this is such a great way of tracking, wouldn't the Light Guards have used it already?" Jules asked.

"There aren't a lot of water fae in the Guard. Most of us aren't interested in fighting anyone," Gawen explained.

"Yeah, I can see that." I nodded my head, thinking about it. It would be hard to fight people, or worse, when you could see their auras and understand exactly what they were feeling. The fear, the anger, the hate. Whatever they were feeling, you would know it. Under those conditions, going up against people like the Dark fae years ago would have been way too traumatizing for most water fae. "Still, wouldn't they keep some water fae on hand for this kind of search and rescue?"

"Well, not everybody can do it. My family used to consult with the Light Guard doing just this kind of work. For some reason, it takes a male water fae and a female water fae. My grandfather used to say it had to do with balance. For us to see the past and bring it into the presents now, it means both aspects have to be able to work together. And for a pair to tap into the waters of time, they need to have some sort of a connection."

"You mean, like romantic? Because I'm not interested in you that way, sorry." I laughed.

"Nothing like that," Gawen said, flushing. "I just meant we have to get along. I know you're not into me, but the moment I saw you in the club that night I felt a connection. That's why I came over and talked to you. So, hey, don't get me wrong, but if you ever are interested I wouldn't turn you down."

Reenah threw a pillow at Gawen. "He pretty much wouldn't turn anybody down."

Gawen grinned. "True enough. You're all attractive girls."

Just then, Jules chat device lit up like the Fourth of July, throwing up holographic sparks in a stunning visual display. Jules' eyes went wide.

"It's Hollis!" she whispered, as if he could hear us.

"You have a special Fourth of July alert for when Hollis calls?" I asked. I don't know why I was surprised. He may have broken her heart, but Jules had been pining over my brother for years. She wasn't one to give up easily.

"Shut up," she muttered, covering up the chat with her hand. That didn't do anything to stop the holograph though, as it continued to shoot past her hand. She must have gotten the newest upgrade. I'd heard it could cast through matter. "I'll just text him back quickly."

She called up the texting screen and typed out a message.

- What's up?

- Are you home?

- Yeah. I got back from my meet a little while ago, why?

-    Nothing. I'll tell you when I see you. Be there in 5.

I had to hand it to Hollis. As much of a jerk as he could be, he did at least try to have good manners. Jules texted him back a thumbs up and turned off the chat.

"Crap," she said looking at me. "This is it. I bet he's looking for you. I better go. You stay here."

"You'll get no argument from me." I could just imagine him hauling me off over his shoulder like some Neanderthal.

"I'll check back with you guys after he's left."

Reenah quirked her lips and hummed to herself.

"You have an idea," Gawen said, looking at her.

"Yeah, I do. Leave your chat on, just make sure it's muted so we can hear you but you can't hear us."

"That's a great idea! Anything specific you want me to ask him?"

"Yeah," I said. "Ask him why he's such an-"

Reenah put a hand on my shoulder. "Silence. Ask what the real story is. There's got to be something he knows, some kind of clue that we can follow."

"Good idea." Jules wiggled her shoulders seductively. "Operation Mata Hari is on."

Chapter 12

"Okay, can you guys hear me alright?"

Jules was standing in front of the device, our apartment visible behind her. Most chats gave the viewer a sort of fisheye view, so you could see 270 degrees. Jules must have set the chat up high on a shelf somewhere in the room, because I could see the door, the main room, the kitchen, everything. I had the stray thought that the apartment looked nice. Decorated in lots of bright blues and turquoise, yellows and oranges, it was a place that I would be comfortable in. I knew that she had taken my taste into account when she'd decorated, instead of assuming I'd be in Aeden forever. Glad one of us had had faith that I'd be allowed to come back.

"I love the place, Jules," I said.

She beamed into the camera. "I'm glad. Alright, I'm going to put you guys on mute now, so I'm not going to be able to hear you, okay?"

The room disappeared from view for a moment as her hand closed over the chat device and then everything came back into view. Gawen reached over to his own chat and expanded the holograph from its standard one-foot wide view to a three-foot wide image hovering over the desk. We could see Jules in the hall mirror, putting on lip gloss.

"Is she primping for your brother?" Reenah asked.

"Looks like it," I said. She made a disgusted sound and I couldn't help but agree. He so did not deserve Jules' best efforts. Forget best. He didn't even deserve her second or third.

Gawen looked confused. "Let's just say he just doesn't deserve her, that's all," I said, enlightening him.

"Agreed," Reenah said. We high-fived each other.

"Don't you think he deserves a second chance? I've seen him at her place a few times, the way he watches her. He's not just checking in on his sister's friend." Gawen said this as if I should feel sorry for Hollis.

"Look, Jules has had it bad for my brother for years, okay? He never noticed. This summer, when he finally realized she was a girl, he treated her just like any of his other admirers from school. He broke her heart, and he didn't even care. He's an ass."

"Wow, tough crowd," Gawen said. Reenah pretended to wipe a tear away from her face, mocking Hollis' pain.

Gawen laughed. "Okay, I got it. Girls rule, boys suck."

"Yup," we girls said in agreement. As if to illustrate our point, Jules stopped pacing nervously and straightened up. Maybe she'd realized that Hollis really didn't deserve her. She headed over to the fridge, muttering under her breath as if she was giving herself some sort of a private pep talk. She poured herself a tall glass of juice and sat at the counter to read through a pile of mail. After a couple more minutes, loud pounding at the door surprised all of us.

"Open up, Jules!" Hollis yelled on the other side.

"Alright, I'm coming. Hold your horses," she called.

Hollis kept banging at the door. "Let me in, I mean it."

"Okay, jeez," she said opening the door slowly. Hollis barged in, flinging the door against the wall as he pushed past Jules. "Hey, watch it! What's your problem?"

"Where is she?" Hollis growled. Khai stepped into the room behind him and I gasped, surprised to see him.

"Check every room," Khai said quietly.

"What the hell do you guys think you're doing?" Jules demanded, planting her hands on her hips. Hollis ignored her, walking through every room turning on lights, throwing open closets, checking cupboards. He even peaked under the dining room table's cloth covering and behind the pillows on the couch. "Hello? I'm asking you guys a question. What the heck is going on?"

Khai just stood there, watching her. Probably trying to see if he could tell if she was pretending innocence. He didn't say a word, despite her repeated questions. After a couple minutes, Hollis finally came back, standing by Khai.

"Nothing." His voice was grim.

Khai massaged the back of his neck, looking defeated and about as exhausted as I had felt before my nap.

"Please tell me you've heard from her," he said bleakly, looking at Jules. Jules crossed her arms and started tapping her foot angrily.

"Heard from who? What are you guys doing here, and why do I feel like I'm living in an ancient communist country or something all of a sudden?"

"Woah, she's good," Reenah muttered. I agreed, but couldn't peel my eyes away from the holo-vid.

"It's Ana," Khai said. "She's run away. We were able to track the gravicycle she took here to one of the campus buildings."

"Then, she must be on her way to see you," Jules said to Hollis.

"She wouldn't be on her way to see me," Hollis said.

"That's the truth," I whispered. None of us had said a word, watching the scene play out on the holo-chat, and even though I knew that Jules had muted us, I'd kept my voice down, afraid that they might sense me somehow.

"Huh. So, what do you mean she's run away? I thought she was having too much fun studying with Airmed to leave Aeden. Why would she leave? You told me she wanted to stay."

I wanted to scream at Hollis, shake him for lying to my best friend, but instead, I just gripped the bedsheets beneath me.

"I may have stretched the truth," Hollis admitted.

"Liar," I hissed under my breath. Gawen looked at me, concerned, and put a comforting hand on mine. His touch calmed me, reminded me to keep breathing.

"Truth is," Khai said, "Ana has been fighting to get back here since the day she left. She wants to go after David."

"So? And you guys have what, been keeping her prisoner?"

"No, not prisoner, just in protective custody," Hollis explained.

"Well, isn't that just something," Jules said, glaring at him. "You just think you're king of the world, don't you Hollis?"

"Hey! You know it wasn't my idea. I don't know what you're trying to imply-"

"Quit it, you two," Khai cut my brother off. "I don't have time for any of your lovers' spats. Ana is missing, don't you get it? All any of us wanted was to keep her safe. The whole thing was her father's idea, so if you want to blame someone, blame Alec." He turned to Jules, imploring. "Do you have any idea where she would go, if it wasn't here to see you?"

"No. Are you sure she didn't want to see her big brother?"

Hollis snorted. "Even I know how unlikely that is. I'd guess I'm one of the last people that Ana wants to see."

"No," Khai said. I'm pretty sure that's me. Dammit!" He turned and punched the wall, putting a fair sized hole in the plaster.

"Okay, easy there. I'm not paying for your foul mood. I had to put down $1,000 security deposit, you know."

"Bill me," Khai said. Hollis put a hand on Khai's shoulder.

"Calm down, man, don't get so worked up. It's going to be okay, no one blames you. We'll find her. Maybe she just hasn't gotten here yet. You know, it could have taken her a while to find Jules' address."

"You're right." Khai cracked his neck, a signal that he was grouping. "I'm going to go back out and keep searching. Hollis, why don't you stay here? Watch the apartment."

"Uh-huh," Jules protested. "No way. He is not staying here in my apartment."

"Fine, I'll wait in the hallway."

"You try it and I'm calling the cops on you. I can't believe you guys were working together, keeping Ana down there against her will. Get out, both of you, out! I see either of you again in this building and I swear to God, I will call the cops and report you for stalking, got it?"

"Fine, gods, we're going," Hollis said holding up his hands and storming out. Khai followed, pausing at the door.

"Please, if you hear from her, will you call us? What she's doing is dangerous." He waited for an answer. Getting none, his shoulders sagged and he exited the apartment.

Jules slammed the door behind him and leaned against it, putting her hands over her face. I thought maybe she was crying, but then after a minute I saw she was desperately trying to contain laughter.

"Wow, she puts on one heck of a performance," Reenah murmured.

"She never had time for drama club with all the sports she did, but when we were little she always got the lead in every school play," I said.

"I can see why," Gawen said with admiration in his voice as we watched Jules grab her chat off the shelf and put it in her ear.

"Okay," she whispered. "They're gone. Did you catch all that?"

"Yeah, we sure did. You were amazing," I said. "I think you really threw them off the scent."

"I hope so. There's only one way to find out though." She walked over to the high tech security monitor by the door. Out by the street, Khai and Hollis were arguing. She didn't turn on the sound so I couldn't hear what they were saying, but after a moment Hollis put up his hood and leaned against the wall. Khai stormed off with purpose, leaving me wondering what they were planning.

Hollis always had a plan.

"He's probably headed back to his own apartment to see if anyone's run into you," Jules mused, echoing my thoughts. "I'm sure they've already alerted campus security to keep an eye out."

"How am I ever going to get out of here now," I wondered out loud.

"I have my ways," said Reenah, looking devious.

"Really? Should I start calling you Spider-Woman? Or maybe you can fly?" Jules asked, disbelief rampant in her voice.

"Not quite. But close enough. You'll see." Reenah winked at me as if to reassure me, but Gawen groaning at my side had the opposite effect.

We watched Jules rummage through dressers and closets, stuffing things into bags. Some, I recognized. My things, sent ahead by mom for school. Warm clothes I'd had no use for in Aeden.

"Okay," she said finally, "I've got some stuff together. Anna, you can go through what I'm grabbing when I get there, pick what you want to bring along."

A minute later, she was standing before us, bags of clothes in hand.

"How many days do you think we should prep for?" I asked, looking at the packs. It looked like she'd brought enough for several weeks.

"Good question," Gawen said, gathering his fine blonde hair into a man bun on top of his head as he thought. "I'd say bring at least enough underwear and socks for five days, go light on the pants and shirts."

"Hey, we know how to pack for a trip," Jules said. "We're just trying to figure out how long we'll be gone. We did the Long Trail, remember?"

"Of course I remember," Gawen retorted. "I'm not a goldfish. But you're girls, right? I mean you guys like to have options and whatever."

Reenah swatted at him over my head and he ducked away, laughing.

Jules dumped out the packs over the bed and we started sorting through our clothes, deciding what to bring. In the end we each picked out one pair of pants, several shirts and pairs of silk long underwear, plus a week's worth of underwear and socks.

Jules held up a wad of cash and handed me half. "Stash this somewhere you won't lose it. Hollis seemed so rabidly intent on finding you, I grabbed the emergency stash of cash my mom gave me last month. I think we should avoid anything that might get us on their radar. Which reminds me – you better go get cleaned up and change into something that actually fits you. We don't want people staring at you like you're some crazy homeless chick."

"Gee, thanks a lot. And hey, Jules?"

"Yeah?"

"I missed you." I gave her a quick hug, stuffed the money into my bra and headed to the bathroom to clean up and change. After a shower, I slipped into my favorite pair of winter shoes, insulated high top sneakers that felt like walking on clouds.

"Okay, I'm ready," I called, coming out of the bathroom. "So tell me again about how we're going to get out of this building without Hollis seeing us?"

"No spoilers, remember?" Reenah patted my cheek lovingly with a devilish gleam in her eye that was in no way reassuring. "All I'm going to tell you is you're in for one hell of a ride."

Chapter 13

The night was inky black. No moon to light our way, just a few trillion stars dancing in the sky. It was the kind of night my mother enjoyed most stargazing outside with a cup of hot cider warming her hands. She often reminded me that when she'd been growing up the light pollution had been so bad, even in the smallest towns like Falls Depot, that you'd barely been able to see the major constellations. Now, the Milky Way radiated across the sky in all its glory, easily visible thanks to global Dark Sky laws that regulated outdoor lighting. Lights couldn't exceed a certain level of lumens, had to fall within certain color ranges, and couldn't point upwards. As a kid, it had been easy for me to learn the constellations, because they actually looked like something, not just five or six points of light creating abstract connect-the-dots.

In a way, I supposed I should be especially grateful tonight. The darkness made it harder to imagine plummeting to my death from five stories. I'd leaned over the edge of the roof a moment ago, swallowed, and retreated a couple feet.

"So, tell me, what's the plan? Because right now I just see a lot of roofs that I can't possibly jump to, and a very, very, distant sidewalk." For the millionth time this month, I wished Ayita was at my side. The Fleet would have been able to clear the distances easily, leaping from roof to roof with no trouble. Her powerful body was made for jumps like this. "Do you have wings hidden under that shirt of yours?"

Reenah laughed heartily. "I wish."

Jules examined Reenah critically. "Yeah, I'd like to know your plan, too. I'm pretty fond of this body."

"So I hear, Legs," Gawen said, using Jules trail name. The moniker had been given to her by some other through hikers as she straddled the state line between Massachusetts and Vermont at the official trail head. A lot of people hiked long distance trails to find themselves – trail names were part of that tradition, nicknames that helped distance you from your everyday life.

Jules winked at Gawen and then became serious again. "Come on, Reenah. Spill."

"What, you don't want to just jump and see how it works out?" Jules and I crossed our arms and looked at Reenah, not amused, while Gawen chuckled and walked over to the wall. Obviously, he knew what was about to happen, and he wasn't about to ruin the surprise.

Reenah sighed. "You guys are no fun at all. Okay. So you asked me before if I could fly. I can't. Wish I could, but so far, no go. But I can sort of float. Think of me as your talking parachute."

"How does that work? If I'm going to do this, I need details," Jules demanded, and I nodded my head.

"Yeah. Details, Reenah."

"Easy. I create an air pocket below me to slow me down. I'm able to thicken the air, make it more resistant for us to pass through. I can call up a little breeze, too, to help us land further away. We'll all jump together, holding hands, and I'll float us over there." She pointed to a park two blocks away.

Jules and I looked at each other, considering. "Okay, that's actually pretty cool," she said, tilting her head.

"You've done this with other people?"

Reenah's smile fell a little. "I've done it with Gawen a couple times. I've practiced a lot jumping off small buildings, though I haven't done any skyscrapers or anything like that. It worked fine with Gawen, we just fell slightly faster."

"Slightly? Like, how much? What's going to happen with four of us?"

Gawen strolled back, clapped a hand on Reenah's shoulder. "We'll be fine. Besides, it's not like we have another option, right? If Reenah says she can do it, trust her."

"It's up to you," Jules said, looking at me. "This is your quest. That makes you team leader."

"What?" I spluttered. "I'm not-"

"You are," Gawen said, cutting me off. "And we trust you. If you want to do this another way, let us know."

Any protests I had within me deflated, and a new sense of resolve burned through me.

"You're right. But we're in this together. Even though I just met some of you, I trust all of you. Everyone gets equal say. Everybody pulls their own weight. And if anyone wants to back out at any time, I'll understand."

Everyone looked at each other, silent communication and resolve passing around the circle in palpable agreement. Finally, Reenah spoke.

"That's not gonna happen, but yeah, thanks. We understand. Now, you ready to fly?"

I took a deep breath. "Let's do it."

We all walked over to the ledge and carefully climbed up, one by one. Somehow, standing those extra few feet higher made the distance to the ground twenty times more daunting. I grabbed Jules' hand, not even bothering to straighten my pack though it listed uncomfortably to one side. I felt like my feet were glued to the ledge. And Reenah expected me to step off? I wasn't sure I could do it.

"Not like that," Reenah said, indicating our linked hands with her chin. "Like this."

She ducked her head to the side, showing us how she and Gawen were holding each other's wrists, locking their arms together. I knew that hold – my father had taught it to me and Hollis at an early age. He'd called it the Survivor's Handshake. I'd never actually needed to use it, but I hoped like hell it would work. I definitely wanted to survive. Jules and I shifted our hands, grasping each other's wrists, and I did the same on the other side with Reenah. Reenah watched to make sure we did it right, then nodded.

"Okay. On the count of three, we jump. No screaming, remember: Hollis is down there, on the other side of the building. We don't want to test how good his hearing is, or how fast he can run. Ready?"

We all nodded.

"One," she whispered. "Two. Three!"

And we jumped, a gentle wind at our backs pushing us away from the building. I was glad we'd locked wrists, because we'd all jumped with varying degrees of strength and distance. My short legs couldn't compete with Jules' powerful soccer-trained limbs, or Gawen's natural masculine build, but the two of them carried Reenah and I forward in an arch. It took a moment before I noticed that we really were falling more slowly than normal. Like a feather on the breeze, we drifted. I lost my fear and started to grin, getting drunk on the sensation of flying. Is this what birds felt like all day long? Because then I was so coming back as a bird in my next life. Any bird. Any size. It didn't matter. As long as I could have more of this.

All too quickly, the ground rushed up at our feet. Had I thought that my shoes felt like walking on clouds? Obviously, I'd been ignorant. Clouds felt like walking on clouds. The ground? It was hard. Cold. I wanted back up in the sky.

"When can we do that again?" I asked, staring up at the stars. I was still holding Reenah's wrist, as if the two of us might take off again at any moment. She gently disentangled herself and Gawen laughed, looking at me.

"Uh-oh. Looks like Reenah's woken your inner wild child."

I glanced at them, and saw Reenah's eyes were gleaming in the night. She looked the way I felt. Exhilarated. "Didn't you like it?" I asked Gawen. I looked at Jules and saw she looked slightly sick.

"Not really. I did a few jumps with her early on, you know, to preserve my manhood, but I can do without it."

"Well, anytime you want to go base-jumping, you call me," I said, looking up at Reenah. "I'm in."

"You've got a deal," she said, grinning down at me. "Now, where to?"

"You know that huge mirrored building near Maisonneuve Market?"

"The bank?" Gawen asked.

"Exactly. Gregor Bank. That's where we're going."

"Wait a minute. You mean the starseed Gregors are the same as-" Gawen trailed off, trying to work it out.

"Yes. The bank is a front for the organization. They've been around a long time, like I said."

"Wow. That's some Illuminati level intrigue right there." Gawen grinned, looking excited. "Well, it's a hike. It'll take us about an hour to walk that far north. Should we take a taxi?"

"And waste the cash I brought? Nah. Let's stretch our legs a little," Jules said, always up for a work-out. My legs were perfectly happy not being stretched any further today, but she had a point about our funds.

"There's a bus stop a few blocks over where we can catch a direct line for free, how about that?" I asked hoping they'd go for the compromise. Everyone agreed it sounded good so we started walking east towards the river.

Reenah and Gawen led the way with Jules and me trailing behind. She'd slowed her long-limbed pace to match my easy stroll.

"So, tell me: how's college? Tell me everything," I demanded.

"Well, finding an apartment without you kind of sucked." She punched me playfully on the shoulder.

"You did a good job. I love what you did with the place. And, you've gotta admit we have great neighbors."

"Oh man, you haven't meant the old man who lives upstairs yet. He walks like Frankenstein's monster, I swear." To illustrate her point, she put her arms out in front of her and started taking long, stiff-legged strides. Then she broke into laughter and I joined her. "Anyhow, you should thank me. I totally restrained myself when I picked out the paint."

"I know you did, thank you," I said, still chuckling. Back home, every single one of her bedroom walls was painted a different wild color, plastered with posters of sports superstars and gorgeous athletes.

"Your mom helped, too. She brought over some of your grandmother's Fiestaware collection when she dropped off all your other stuff."

"Really, she sent the Fiestaware? That's so awesome! What colors?" I know, it's probably hugely dorky how excited I get over bright pottery, but it's an inherited obsession in my family. Our love of Fiestaware runs deep, an inescapable blood addiction.

"Pretty much the whole rainbow. She sent all your clothes, too, like I said. I put them away for you."

"You didn't have to do that. You could have just left the suitcases in my room."

"I tried that for a few days, but it just felt weird. I thought if I arranged your room, then I'd feel like you were almost there, you know? It almost worked. Sometimes I was able to convince myself you were in your room, studying or reading, or whatever geek-thing you would normally be doing."

I hip-checked her. "Thanks a lot. But I know what you mean. I missed you, too."

"I still can't believe that you were stuck in Aeden all this time against your will. I had no idea. I feel terrible, like I should have known."

"It's not your fault. How could you have? I mean, it's like my entire family has gone crazy or something."

Jules chewed on her lip. "I don't know. I wouldn't say they're crazy. They just care about you, you know?"

I snorted. "Did you know that Khai tased me?"

"What?" she asked incredulously. "When?"

"On our way to Aeden. My dad called him, told him what had happened to David and to get me down to Airmed's by any means necessary. Of course, when I heard what had happened I wanted to come back here, help find David right away. Khai and I argued, and he tased me," I said. The memory of it made my mouth taste bitter. "One moment we were fighting in the woods, the next, I was waking up in a bed at Airmed's under house arrest."

"That's messed up."

"I didn't talk to him for weeks after that."

"He's lucky you ever talked to him again. I can't believe Khai would do that to you."

"I can still hardly believe it myself. I didn't really want to forgive him, but you know how hard it is to stay mad at Khai."

"I guess." She looked at me doubtfully, as if she would have had no problem carrying my grudge to the grave.

"Anyhow, I knew they would never let me off Airmed's property unless they thought I was going to behave. So I started letting Khai train with me, smiled at some of his jokes. I stopped complaining about being there, at least, I tried my best. And I was right. After a few weeks, Airmed finally let Khai escort me to the forest to collect acorns. She's probably kicking herself now," I said, grinning. "I ran off the first chance I got."

"How'd you get away?" Her eyes had gone round with curiosity.

"I'm not proud to admit it, but I kind of knocked him out by hitting him over the head with a rock."

Jules gasped. "It was a small rock," I explained in a rush. "And I did check him to make sure he would be okay."

Jules laughed. "Of course you did. As if you would do anything else," she said, shaking her head. "Well, he's obviously not hurt, so it's not like you need to feel guilty about it."

"Then can you tell me why I do?" I pleaded, only half-kidding.

Jules shrugged. "You're a lover, not a fighter."

"I'm not sure if I love Khai anymore."

"That's just anger talking. He's family. You'll never stop loving him."

"I guess. Speaking of love, what about you?" I asked, deciding to turn the tables. "What's going on with you and Hollis?"

"He's stopped by a few times, giving me updates on how you were doing in Aeden. Apparently, he wasn't telling me the whole story, though."

I looked at Jules' face, the way several expressions shifted across it. Annoyance to anger, then pain to sadness, and then annoyance again.

"You still like him?"

Jules sighed. "I know, I probably shouldn't. He almost broke my heart, you know?"

"Almost? I'd say he did a pretty good job."

Her lips scrunched up in a pout as she agreed with me. Her voice turned heavy, wistful. "But we really did have something, you saw it, right? We connected, boy, did we connect. I mean I could have-"

I held up a hand to stop her. "Please, let's not go there, okay? I don't think I can stomach hearing about you and my brother making out, seriously. But I know what you are saying. He did act differently with you. Like he really saw you. More than any other girl I've seen him with. I was just as surprised as you when he broke it off so suddenly."

She sniffed, and I realized my best friend was about to cry.

"Aw, Jules, don't do that. He's not worth it, okay? If he can't see how great you are, he doesn't deserve you."

Unfortunately, my words had the opposite effect I'd intended, and she wound up bawling in my arms.

"Dammit Ana," she hiccupped. "Why can't he just love me the way I love him?"

Silently, I cursed my brother. What was I supposed to say? He'd always had a love 'em and leave 'em attitude when it came to dating. I'd never seen him settle on anyone for more than a couple days. Something about the way he'd been with Jules, though, had been different. If I knew my brother, and sometimes I felt like I might, he'd liked her enough to get well and truly spooked. I didn't want to tell Jules that, though. What if I was wrong? What if I got her hopes up for nothing?

So I said what every good friend says at a moment like this.

"He's an idiot. Forget about Hollis, Jules. You can do so much better."

Again, my word failed, and she bawled harder. I was just debating what to do next when Gawen came sprinting back to us.

"What's the holdup? Reenah's stalling the bus for us, but they're not going to wait forever."

"Crap," Jules swore, wiping the tears from her face. "I'm fine. Come on!"

We sprinted for the bus at the end of the block and ran up the steps, laughing as the adrenaline pumped through us. The bus was mostly empty, just a few old men in one row and a mom with a little kid reading a book up front. We stumbled towards the back, taking our seats, and rode the rest of the way in silence. When we got off at Maisonneuve, the bus driver looked at us with concern.

"You sure you kids want to get off here? Nothing around but offices and shops, and everything's all closed up now. Word is there've been some break-ins in the district recently."

"Don't worry, sir, we're here for a research project," Reenah said sweetly, and the driver relaxed.

"Okay. Well, you kid's stay safe now. I'll be driving back this way in an hour. If you need a ride, you just flag me down."

"We will, thank you, sir," I assured him, and gave Reenah a little shove towards the exit.

Chapter 14

We all held our breath until the bus moved off and then the dam burst, laughter spilling forth.

"Oh my god, Reenah, that face!" Jules wheezed, batting her eyelashes. "Oh no, sir, we're just good little students."

"If he only knew! We're the ones about to some B&E!" I giggled.

Gawen sobered up. "But those break-ins he was talking about. He probably meant the bank, right? I mean, what else could it be."

I swallowed. "You're right. I guess we're gonna find out, either way."

Gawen nodded, looking towards me, but not at me. I guessed he was reading my aura, the way most people read expressions. "You sure you're ready for this?"

"Don't I look ready?" I challenged.

"More or less," he said, winking at me. "Don't worry, we're here to make up that last bit."

"Don't mind Gawen, luv," Reenah said, throwing her arm around his shoulder. "He can't help being 100-percent honest, all the time. You'll get used to it."

"No filter," Gawen said, apologizing.

"Which is why we love you," Jules said, smacking her lips against his cheek. "Now let's go do this thing."

As a group, we turned and looked at the bank. It's mirrored surface gleamed black, reflecting stars above and the dim street lights along the avenue. It reminded me of black ice, that most dangerous kind of ice on roads, the kind of ice frozen so clear on a pond you could see through it, whether it was two feet thick or two inches. I remembered one year when I was ice skating with my family: I'd seen the fish looking up at me through the clear ice, their large mouths opening and closing hungrily, wondering if I was going to drop some worms down to them through the ice. Of course, I hadn't.

Unfortunately, this mirrored surface did not share the revealing qualities of black ice. Looking at the building, I had no way to tell what waited for us inside. A small sign taped to the front entrance declared the premises "temporarily closed for renovations."

"What now? How do we get in?" I wondered.

"We can't just break in," Gawen said, thinking out loud. "A place like this has gotta have some kind of alarm system."

"For all the good it did them," I muttered.

Jules looked at Reenah. "I don't suppose you can fly to the top of the building, jimmy the lock on the roof?"

"I wish. I haven't figured out how to go up yet, just down."

Gawen rubbed his hands together, looking more excited than the rest of us. "Time for some reconnaissance. Let's walk around the building, get off the street where someone might report us for suspicious activity."

I started to wish I had someone like my dad or grandmother with us, someone who'd been trained in the lost arts of breaking and entering.

"Don't look so worried," Gawen said, throwing an arm around my shoulder as we walked. "Even a fortress like this has to have a back entrance, a place for deliveries and emergency exits."

We turned the corner, entering a wide alley. Gawen was right. A large sign lit in red and white marked the side entrance, a set of heavy fire doors near a large dumpster. Of course the Gregors would have needed a place to bring in food and other supplies for the people who lived there. They would have wanted to keep up the pretense of being a regular business, without raising any red flags.

"Now what?" I asked sourly. "We still can't get inside. Not without setting off some kind of alarm."

Gawen didn't look concerned. "I'm not convinced we need to. Remember what I said about how we can tap into the imprint of a place? Well, the warpers got the starseeds out somehow, and I'm doubting it was through the front doors."

"So we do it here, right out in the open? That balancing thing you were talking about?"

"Yup." He grinned down at me. "You're not nervous, are you?"

I pursed my lips, mildly tempted to try out some of my mom's Krav Maga on his cocky face. I choked back my annoyance, knowing Gawen was just being Gawen and my nerves were getting to me. Self-assured and carefree. It wasn't his fault that I lived on the opposite end of the spectrum. "No."

"Good." Gawen's face turned serious. "I want you to feel yourself as the birthplace of all that is good and pure."

"I don't know how," I complained.

Behind me, Jules laughed. "If you asked me a few months ago, I would have said that Anna was as pure as the driven snow, but now-"

Gawen shushed her. "Quiet. Like I said before, this isn't about her body, this is about her purity as a vessel of the creative energy of Anansanna, the Divine light that makes all fae, fae. I want you to focus on that energy." Gawen looked at me intensely. "Focus on your womb or your heart or whatever. Zero in on that purity, that energy you have within you that allows you to act as an anchor for all the sun's power."

"What are you going to be concentrating on," I asked.

"I'll be concentrating on my masculine side."

Reenah snorted.

"Look, I do have one you know."

"I don't know. Your hair is so pretty," Jewels gushed, mocking him.

"Whatever." Even in the dim light of the alley, his blush was evident. "Concentrate on anchoring and driving the creative power I need. Once I can feel you channeling it, I'll work on pushing it out into this place, breaking through the boundaries of space and time so we can see what happened here."

"Okay. I'm not going to claim that I understand everything that's supposed to be happening here, but if you can actually get this to work, well, that'll be pretty cool."

"I'll take that as a vote of confidence," Gawen said, pleased. "Come on, everybody join hands. Jules, you and Reenah stand between Ana and me. You'll be acting as batteries, giving us some extra juice."

"Sounds like fun," Jules whispered under her breath and I squeezed her hand.

"Be nice," I admonished, secretly grateful I wasn't the only one expressing some nerves. I looked across at Gawen. "And then?"

"Close your eyes. I'm going to walk us through some visualizations. Ana, I want you to start by reaching deep into yourself. Bring up all your curiosity, everything you want to know, okay?"

It wasn't difficult. I'd always had an insatiable curiosity, a yearning to know more than I was taught. It's what had led me to love literature from all genres and ages.

"Perfect." Gawen must have been watching me, reading my aura to see how I was progressing. "While you're doing that, Reenah and Jules, I want you to imagine light flowing through you, around the circle, from left to right. Exactly, just like that. Perfect. That's a good energy flow, can you guys feel that?"

It took me a minute to acclimate to the heightened energy pulsing through me like waves on a beach, but I could. Not the searing energy of Anansanna, but something earthier, grittier. More tangible. Living energy from the four of us. If I tried hard enough, I could even taste the energy of each of us in separate threads. Gawen's incredibly light and bright. Reenah's bitter cold, fresh. Jules and her earthy energy, slower, but sweet and rich.

"Jules, you have magic in you," I blurted out, surprised. She dropped my hand, looking just as shocked.

"I do?"

"Definitely," Reenah confirmed.

"What does that mean?"

"I don't know," I said. "But we'll figure it out. Maybe there's a reason you've always liked Hollis so much."

"Why?" she asked.

"Your energy, it's earthy..."

"And so is Hollis," she mused, picking up the thread.

"Like attracts like," Gawen said, nodding. "Well, sometimes." He looked at Reenah, distracted. "Come on, everybody stay connected. We can't lose this energy. Let's see what information we can get from the door."

He pulled us over to stand in front of the door in a line, hands linked.

"Ana, put your free hand on the door. Allow yourself to anchor the energy imprint stored there, and we'll pull it in. That's it! Keep going. Stay connected." Gawen went quiet, his eyes closed in pain. After a few moments, he spoke with a grimace. "Oh wow. Okay, Ana, I'm going to open up myself to you so you can see what I'm seeing. Ana, imagine yourself walking into the scene. Let it play out, like a story."

"Doesn't look like such a great story," I said.

Gawen looked up, clearly trying not to think about it – probably an impossibility when it was playing through his head. I closed my eyes and tried to stay open to whatever he was about to show me.

I wasn't sure what I was expecting to see.

I guess I'd figured that it would be like watching security footage, maybe starting from the most recent history of this spot and then rewind from there. Instead, I felt punched in the gut as a man dragged a woman by her hair through the door.

Through me.

I got to experience the emotional pain of the woman and the glee of the man, the pain of the building so intense I thought I might break in half. It had felt itself to be a safe place. It had cared for all the tiny bodies within it, sheltering them. Enjoying them. It had thought it was impenetrable, but now it was being robbed and violated. I felt its pain in that moment, and its sadness now. The emptiness and loss if harbored. It held no love for the warpers, the beings who had invaded its halls bringing violence and fear.

Before I could regain my breath, a dark-haired woman was pushed through me, a whimpering child clinging to her neck. The pain continued, relentless. We must have watched at least thirty starseeds being escorted or carried outside by the warpers. The pain was virulent, like nothing I'd ever experienced before. No minor empathic headache had prepared me for the scope of these emotions. And the building had stored them all, taking it on as its own. Suddenly, I had a new respect for inanimate objects. I would never look at a coffee mug the same way again. My mother had always told me that everything was alive, that spirit ran through everything, but I'd never really believed it until now.

Yet for all the pain, I picked up nothing from the warpers. No indication of their final goal or destination, no errant thoughts or conversations about who was in charge or why they were doing this. The warpers, as a group, were single-minded. Hateful and enjoying their mission, looking no further than the box truck behind me that would take them – where? For what purpose? This was getting us nowhere.

I broke hands, disconnecting myself from Gawen's vision. "I saw them, the people they took. Can we connect to the truck, the one they got loaded into? See where it went?"

Gawen shook his head. "We can try, but it's unlikely that will have left an imprint where it was parked."

"How come?" Jules asked, cocking her head.

"The land has to really be severely impacted to hold memories like what Ana and I just watched. The alley is a public space, it won't have had the same level of connection to what happened. And the truck, well, it looked like a rental."

"But that's perfect!" Reenah exclaimed. "A rental truck should have records we can track."

"Yeah, but from what Hollis told me, all the surveillance feeds were scrubbed." Jules crossed her arms over her chest, shrugging and looking cold.

"Okay, and you believed him?" Rihanna asked skeptically.

"It's not so much that I believe him, but it makes sense. The warpers have good tech. They've been hiding in plain sight for years. They would have covered their tracks," I said.

Gawen started pacing. "That would be the smart thing to do. For all their vileness, the warpers seemed well organized. They weren't worried about getting caught."

"Yeah? Maybe they're just psycho enough not to care," Reenah quipped. "They sound like the kind of people who go looking for fights."

"Nah. I don't think so," Gawen disagreed. "This wasn't just some random attack, right Ana?" He looked at me and I frowned. "They have a plan. We just need to find out what it is."

"How?" I countered. "We've already tapped the building. Which, by the way, was super weird. It had emotions, I swear. How is that possible?"

"When buildings take on emotions, they become almost alive. The frequency of their vibration can create positive or negative portals of energy, entrances into other realities or aspects of this dimension."

"Oh, come on." I rolled my eyes, but inside, I believed him. I'd felt that building. I'd experienced how awake it was.

"Seriously. I'm not making this stuff up. I know it sounds crazy, but if you read up on basic physics it's all spelled out. These portals, they can even suck in beings from other worlds, bring in things that you don't even want to think about. Trust me, I've seen it myself." He looked down, remembering something he clearly didn't want to talk about. "Anyhow, anything that is used for the same purpose for a long time – toys, jewelry, whatever, they will take on energy. If there was love in a building, it becomes a haven. If there isn't, it might become resentful. And if bad things happen there, well…"

"Like a poltergeist? Is that where that comes from?" Jules asked.

"Sometimes, yeah. A lot of spiritual philosophers called them thought-forms. Beings that derived from our thoughts."

"Kind of like how you're able to manipulate reality with your energy as a fae," Jules exclaimed.

"Exactly. It's one of the reasons a lot of us have always believed that humans are more like us than the Light Council led us to believe. Just because you guys didn't have lots of active powers didn't mean that you weren't able to connect with the land or awaken sleeping spirits. Many of you were able to see auras, despite your supposed lack of powers. I've always imagined that even without the Flare, humanity would have become like us eventually. It was already happening, the massive spiritual awakening that was going on in your world, that whole 'New Age' movement. It was no coincidence."

"Spiritual lessons aside, can we get on with this? My buns are starting to freeze," Reenah complained.

Gawen laughed. "Anything you want, princess. Let's get this door open."

"But how?" Jules said, clearly getting cranky. "Won't these doors be wired?"

"Most likely. It's too bad we don't have a fire fae here to fry the circus," Gawen mused, looking at me.

"I am not calling Khai," I ground out.

"No one's asking you to. There's something I've been wanting to try out for a while now, but I haven't had the power to do it on my own. But together..." He trailed off, turning to look at the doors, considering.

"Spit it out. What?" I asked.

"What if we could channel some water into the circuits? Wouldn't that fry the circuits as well as any lightning could?"

"Water-bending? I thought that existed only in movies."

"Oh, it can be done, though it's more difficult than you would think. I've never mastered it. But two of us working together, I think we stand a chance."

"Well, I'm game. What do we do? Steal water from the air?"

"I wish," Gawen said. "No, we'll need a water source."

"Hold on." Jules ran back towards the street and picked up a half-empty bottle from the ground. "Will this do?"

"That's not water, Jules," I said. "It's soda."

126

"Close enough. It'll work. At least, it should." Gawen took the bottle from Jules. "Okay, so this is how it works. Water travels the path of least resistance, right?"

"Right," we all answered. Suddenly I was having flashbacks to my mid-grade science classes, complete with the approving teacher.

"Alright. So we're not going to attempt anything crazy, like levitating water. We're just going to help it do what it does best." He led us over to the door where we stared at the bolt lock. "Reenah, can you thicken the air around the lock here to form a sort of pocket for the water to sit in?"

He gestured under the lock and around its edges in a cupped shape.

"I can try." She placed her hands around the lock and closed her eyes, concentrating.

Gawen took my hand in his and started pouring the dark liquid over the lock until the bottle was empty. It pooled around the fixture like a bubble. He dropped the bottle and put his hand over Reenah's covering the cup she was forming. Concentration wrinkled his brow. At first, nothing happened, but then I saw the fluid level begin to fall, a small trickle disappearing into the lock.

"It's working!" Jules cheered in a hushed voice.

"Anna, I want you to think of the wires and circuits connected to this door. Help me channel that image to the water."

"Okay, I'll try." I really had no idea what the door looked like inside its hollow steel core or how the locking mechanism was laid out. I decided to just trust my intuition and go with the flow like water. The inky cola had vanished from sight, all of it now inside the door. I could feel a dim connection to the liquid and imagined it traveling quickly along wires like a burning fuse.

"How long do you think we should wait?" Reenah whispered. "How will we know when it's worked?"

Gawen shrugged, his intense expression undiminished. I took that as my cue to keep concentrating. The seconds ticked by and I felt like I could hear a loud clock overhead going tick-tock, tick-tock, tick-tock. I'd always thought I was a patient person, but the waiting was killing me. Any moment now, I expected someone to walk by the alley and call us out for loitering.

I tried to put my worries from my mind and stay focused. The alley had gone completely silent and still, all of us hardly daring to breathe, not moving a muscle. A muted sizzle and pop practically jolted me out of my skin.

I leapt back from the noise, letting go of Gawen's hand as I dropped into a defensive stance. Reenah stood ready to fight, too. Gawen and Jules just looked at us both. Gawen raised his shoulder and quirked an eyebrow.

"Sounds like it worked," he said. Reenah and I looked at each other, realizing we may have overreacted, and dissolved into a fit of giggles.

"I guess the tension kind of got to me. I wasn't really expecting it to work," I apologized, feeling sheepish. "I'll never doubt you again."

"As family, I reserve that right. Now step aside," Reenah said, waving Gawen out of the way. She leaned down towards the lock and blew gently into the tumbler. White cobwebbed veins of ice spread over the silvery metal as if she were Jack Frost himself. I could only imagine that the same was happening within the door. Looking satisfied, she straightened and stepped back to aim a fierce side kick at the lock. Fractured pieces of metal flew inwards and her smile widened.

"Let's go, ladies." She grabbed the door handle and pulled it open, leading us inside. Impressed, we followed, Gawen grumbling at the rear about not being a lady.

A glance at the security system on the wall confirmed an electrical short in the system, a telltale smudge of dark soot on the wall above it.

"Looks like we're good, Gawen said.

"Do you think anyone's monitoring the system?" Jules wondered. "Won't they notice something's wrong?"

"I don't think so," I answered. "I think the Gregors do everything in-house. Staying off-grid as much as possible is probably why no one noticed what was happening here until it was too late."

"Still, we shouldn't waste any time lingering." Gawen said.

I was happy to agree just being inside the building made the hair on my arms stand up and my stomach roll. I didn't want to be here. I could feel the energy around me, the residual unhappiness. I'd never been in a haunted house before, at least not that I'd noticed but the creep factor here oozed from every surface. Regardless, we couldn't leave until we found something, any breadcrumb that would lead us to David and the others.

A quick scan of the area revealed nothing different from what we had seen outside so we walked out into the main lobby and linked hands again. The show started, a team of warpers walking in through the front door pretending to be wayward tourists. Two of them had taken out the security guards like vicious efficiency experts, wasting no movement, while another had walked off towards the way we'd come in, returning with more warpers. One of the newcomers, a voluptuous woman dressed in a white catsuit, walked over to the front desk and picked up a microphone. Her voice flowed through the building, rich and cultured, smooth like a vanilla milkshake.

"Attention, this is not a drill. Please proceed to the lobby and await further instructions. I repeat, this is not a drill." She set down the mic and flipped her long silver hair over her shoulder, smiling at the man next to her. "Like bringing in lambs for the harvest."

Even though I was already in the lobby, I wanted to go there so badly. I wanted her instructions. Needed them. Realization set my nerves tingling.

"She's a speaker," I murmured.

"You're right," the man said to the woman in white, his back to me. "But some of the people in this building will be able to resist you, as hard as that may be for you to imagine."

"Nonsense, no one can resist me." She gave him an alluring smile.

"I can."

Her smile turned feral and she glared back at him. He laughed, his amusement catching me off-guard. I'd heard that voice before, in my dreams.

Turn around, I willed him silently. *Please, turn around.* I needed to see his face. I wanted so badly to let go of my friend's hands, walk around the memory, examine him; but I didn't know what that would do to the re-creation. I wasn't sure if the vision would cut out if I disconnected from the group, and the last thing I wanted to do was interrupt it. Impatiently, I waited.

The elevator dinged, unleashing footsteps and murmured voices behind me. The first wave of starseeds had answered the woman's call.

Chapter 15

"What's this all about?" A man strode ahead of the group from the elevator, looking irritated and self-assured, a dangerous combination.

"Marcus," the woman purred. "I was hoping I would see you today."

"Elaine?" His eyes widened as if he couldn't believe what he was seeing.

"Hello, darling. Long time no see."

"I thought you were dead."

"Clearly not," she said, raising an eyebrow. But your ship, the reports said-."

"A convenient story, yes. I was tired of the Gregors watching my every move."

Pain flickered through his eyes. He had loved her, I could feel it.

"I mourned you. How could you choose them over us?"

"What can I say? The benefits are great," she sneered. "Now, kneel. On your knees, all of you!"

"Elaine, you can't do this," he pleaded as he collapsed to his knees. "You know it's not right."

"Don't talk to me about right. All you ever wanted was for me to deny who I really am, but here's the thing dear. I like having people listen to me. I like being the center of attention, I always have. Debate team, drama club, it's just my nature." She had walked over to him, and was running her hands through his hair like a lover. At the last instant, she grabbed it tight in her fist, yanking his head back as she bent down, a wild look in her eyes. "Now sleep."

She released him as he fell backwards, unconscious, and waved a hand towards the rest of the assembled starseeds. "You heard me. Sleep!"

Delight was clear in her cackle and I felt like I was watching a modern adaptation of Sleeping Beauty. *Where's the dragon,* I wondered cynically.

"See, I told you. Piece of cake." She looked pleased with herself, but some of the warpers carrying the unconscious starseeds outside had a few choice words for her, grumbling about having to carry sleeping prisoners.

The man from my dream turned, his shaved head covered with a week's worth of stubble, and locked an arm around her.

"Elaine, you are a prize among women."

"Thank you, Phineas."

"Still, just in case, I'll head upstairs now." He motioned for part of the team to follow him. "I'll sweep the floors, make sure everyone is complying with your influence."

Her face soured. "You still doubt me, after all these years."

"Nonsense, my dear. I've never doubted you, not once. But we must not underestimate our foes either."

He landed a gentle kiss on her temple and strode off, assigning several men to sweep the stairs while his team entered the newly vacated elevators. Elaine watched him go, and then turned her attention to the zombified newcomers.

"Welcome, my pretties!" She clapped her hands together with glee as they approached. "Please, let's see some smiles on those faces." The starseeds lips curved upwards, some baring their teeth in feral threat. She tsked, unimpressed.

"You'll have to do better than that. Kneel! That's right, every one of you. You will not resist us. You will not try to fight or escape. You will do as you are told. You will sit quietly in the truck, and over the coming days you will come to know who I am as we all get to know one another."

One woman looked up at Elaine, a smirk on her face. "Oh, I know who you are. Believe me, I'll never forget."

"Hello, Sasha. So nice to see you again. I see you're just as insipid as ever."

"And I see you're just as nasty as you were before. Still trying to impress all the boys?" Sasha hissed.

Elaine looked at the man behind her, her face betraying no emotion. "Bind this one extra tight. She has such small hands. Wouldn't want her wriggling away like the worm she is."

Sasha cried out as he secured the ropes, twisting them into an impossible knot around her wrists, and yanked her to her feet by the ends.

"Sorry, not sorry," Elaine said, giving a dainty shrug. "I can't wait to have front row seats when our scientists work their magic on you. You're going to wish you never reported me."

Sasha's face went as white. "I was your teacher. What did you expect me to do?"

For a moment doubt flickered across Elaine's face, but then she shook her head, banishing whatever thought had tried to take hold. "I suppose I expected you to take my side. To stand up for me, give me another chance."

"You were abusing your powers, hurting people. There was nothing I could do. You wasted every chance we gave you."

"So you allowed them to throw me into the street. Where did you think I would go? Whatever I am now, it's your fault." Elaine looked at the guard by her teacher's side and delivered the final blow. "Take her away."

"You'll pay for this Elaine," Sasha yelled over her shoulder as the guard dragged her away.

Elaine laughed heartedly, like she knew that would never happen.

I remembered what David had told me about how starseeds were only given one or two chances to redeem themselves if they were found abusing their powers. I knew the Gregors believed in rehabilitation. David said that after the first offense, a starseed would undergo intense moral and technical training programs. If they broke the rules again, they were out. The Gregors believed using your powers to harm others for fun warped the user permanently, that at a certain point a warper was irredeemable. But as a fae, I knew that there was always light in the dark, you just had to find it. In one single act, my mother had rewired the races of humanity and fae to shun the kind of darkness the warpers harbored. Wars had ended. Crimes were practically non-existent. Were the Gregors not trying hard enough?

Elaine certainly seemed to think that she could have been saved.

I wasn't sure. She took a little too much pleasure in the strength of her influence over others. But then again, in her mind, she was punishing the people who had failed her. She'd had a teacher here once. Friends. Maybe if they had all come together, tried harder, they could have saved her.

Or, maybe not. It was all speculation now.

At this very moment, Elaine and her friends were using their power to transform innocents, children, into warpers. It wasn't right. People should always be given a choice. I didn't care how victimized the warpers felt, no one deserved to be treated this way. Forcing people to kneel and grovel? The warpers were bullies of the worst kind.

I was so lost in my own thoughts, I hadn't been paying attention to the vision. A whole new crop of starseeds had arrived. I watched Elaine assess each of them as they knelt before her. My breath caught as my eyes ranged over the back row. I would have known that sandy head of hair anywhere.

"David!" I cried, lunging toward him.

"Ana, no!" Gawen cried as I broke from our circle, letting go of Jules' and Reenah's hands. As soon as I let go, the image of my beloved shimmered like the mirage it was. Elaine began to fade out, and I hurried back to the circle, grabbing my friends' hands.

"You can't break the circle," Gawen warned. "They're not real."

I ignored him, staring at David, watching his bowed head. The way his shoulders sagged, he looked so defeated. It broke me. I wanted to scream, cry, wail.

I did none of those things. I renewed a vow. *I will find you*, I swore, even as a brute of a man with a long jagged scar running down one cheek cuffed David on the ear.

"Get up," he said. The man yanked David to his feet and dragged him outside, David's eyes glassy and unseeing. By his own admission, David had never been a fighter. He believed in goodness and due process. Before heading on an extended sabbatical to walk the Long Trail, he's worked as a mayor's aide in Philadelphia.

I could see the toll this was taking on him, just one more piece of his value system being torn away. Even though David was older than me, in a lot of ways I was more jaded. Maybe it was all the classic lit I loved to read, but I understood the darker side of things. It didn't matter that we lived in a utopia now. Like any historian versed in ancient wars, I knew how jealousy and greed could corrupt hearts. Watching the warpers twisted souls wring the joy out of David's countenance, I felt like I was witnessing mean children spray-paint a puppy. Would they train him to bite and attack, too, twist him to their ways?

No. I shook my head in denial. I wouldn't let that happen. I couldn't.

"I need to know where they are taking him." My eyes pleased with Gawen's.

"Just wait, he said. "We need to see how this plays out. Maybe Elaine says something, or that guy who went to scope the building.

Sighing impatiently, I complied with his rational thinking. Unfortunately, nothing much happened. The warpers returned carrying several unconscious starseeds, complaining about the resistance they'd encountered on the fourth floor, and then they'd laughed and left.

The foyer went silent and still. The daylight of the vision turned dim with reality.

We released hands. I felt drained, and it was all for nothing.

"This can't be a dead end, it just can't be," I said, kicking a hapless dust mote.

"Maybe it's not. Let's go upstairs, check the fourth floor," suggested Jules. "The guys said the starseeds were difficult up there. People tend to say things in the heat of the moment, happens all the time in soccer."

"Good idea," Reenah said with false cheer. I could tell they were all trying to keep my spirits up, so I offered a weak smile. There wasn't any point in bringing them down with me. Though of course if I'd really believed that, I wouldn't have brought them here in the first place.

We rode the elevator silently upstairs. According to the signage in the lobby, this floor housed the management offices and conference rooms. There were no signs of recent life, but thankfully there was no blood, either. A few overturned chairs, a broken picture frame – not much to suggest any major struggles. At the end of the hall, we found the office for the director, a sign reading Cliff Collet. The office seemed undisturbed, except for a lone pen lying on the thick carpet, as if someone had dropped it on their way out the door.

I leaned down, picked it up. Wide open and unprepared for the onslaught, a wave of emotions slithered through me. I collapsed, my knees folding in on themselves. Anger, sadness, regret: all tied up with a neat little bow named defiance. A hand on my shoulder brought me out of it.

I opened my eyes without even realizing I had closed them in anguish.

"Are you okay? What did you see?"

I didn't say anything at first, ignoring Gawen's question as I breathed in and out – too fast, too hard.

He squeezed my shoulder and I blinked up at him owlishly. "Awful. I felt awful. Something bad happened

137

here, I know it. This pen belonged to the director. I think he was holding it when they came to take him."

"Okay, then, hand it to me," Gawen said coolly. His calm voice helped me wall off some of the emotions riding through me, allowed me to catch my own breath. "Let's form another circle."

We linked hands again. This time the energy flowed immediately. I didn't even have to think about what we were doing. Holding hands was like resetting a breaker. All of a sudden the energy was moving, blasting through us. Holding the pen, Gawen zeroed in on the etheric memory and I followed like we are on pony parade.

It happened so quickly, my body felt like it had been turned inside out. It took me a moment to bring the scene before me into focus, I was so busy trying not to throw up. That alone threw me for a moment – could I even throw up in a vision? My physical reaction made me think about what Gawen had said about breaking through time and space. Had we actually stepped back through time to watch these things happen somehow? If we were here, even in the smallest of ways, could I do something to save David now, before it even happened? I shook my head, relegating the thought to the trash heap. If that was possible, if we were really here, the people would have given us some indication. We were just spectators. This was a non-interactive journey. David had talked about what it was like when he dream traveled, and I figured this must be something similar.

An irritated protest drew my attention away from my thoughts.

"What is the meaning of this? What do you people want?" Collet demanded. He was a handsome older man, his dark hair growing gray around the temples. A pair of thick-rimmed glasses gave him the air of benevolent authority.

"You'll have to come with us to find out. Don't pretend you didn't hear the orders. Time to go." Phineas motioned for Collet to get moving.

"I'm not going anywhere with you. You think that a little bit of mind control can do anything to me? Do you know who my best friend is?"

"We know all about your connection to Mrs. Hale. Rumor is she and her husband have both retired."

"You think that will save you? Callie will come for me, you know she will and when she does-"

"Yeah, yeah. I will pay the ultimate price. I've heard it all before. Ethan Hale never scared me, and neither does his traitor wife. Missy Crimholt read me the riot act when I got kicked out of the Dallas office but look at me, alive and kicking. Now, like I said, you really need to come with us."

Collet looked at the pen in his hands, considering.

"I don't think so." He raised one hand and pointed it at Phineas. Suddenly, he was holding a gun, not a pen like I had thought.

"Don't you try your holo-tricks on me," Phineas drawled blandly. "You think I didn't notice that you were holding a pen just a minute ago? Now, if you want to talk about guns, this one here; this is a real beauty." He drew a huge pistol from his belt and aimed it at Cliff, releasing the safety at the same time. Cliff winced and dropped the gun, the gleaming metal morphing to gold-inlaid burl wood as the pen hit the floor.

Phineas cackled. "Elaine said you weren't much of a fighter."

"Elaine Carhartt?" Cliff asked, surprised.

"Who else? You know, she begged to be in charge of this operation. I guess she felt like she had a score to settle with this office. I can't imagine why."

Collet stalled. "Elaine's parents, they're still alive. You know, I could arrange a meeting-"

"I don't think Miss Carhartt is interested in traveling to any further north at the moment. If she changes her mind, I'm sure she'll let you know. After all, you're going to have plenty of time to get reacquainted once we arrive in Salem."

"Salem, Massachusetts?" Cliff looked confused. "Why there?"

"You Gregors really are all the same. You don't pay attention to anything unless it has to do with your own agenda. Salem has been a warping stronghold since it was founded. At first, there were just a couple of us, but over the years our population grew."

"The witches? Those were warpers?"

Phineas laughed, truly amused. "Those hapless twits? No. Our girls accused the people who were starting to suspect our own. It was easy. A little mind control here, some illusions there. Meddling women hanging there and there. It was beautiful. I would have loved to have seen it, wouldn't you?"

Cliff looked repelled. "My friends will find me. My husband won't rest until he gets me back."

Phineas cocked his head to one side, a slow grin twisting across his face.

"Then I hope he's in really good shape, because he's in for the run of his life."

Chapter 16

Jules was rooting around in the kitchen cabinets, looking for a road-snack while we debated our next step. There wasn't much to discuss. Salem remained our best bet, our only bet. Scans throughout the rest of the building hadn't turned up any other leads.

"There's an Eastie in forty minutes going to Boston," Reenah said, referring to the high-speed rail system that connected all the major cities along the east coast of the North American States as she scanned her chat's holo-screen. "From there, Salem is just a short drive."

"The terminal's a good half hour walk from here. We better head out," Gawen said, looking at Jules.

"I'm coming, I'm coming," she muttered, backing out from the pantry and holding up several boxes of granola bars. "Look what I-"

Gawen held up a hand, cutting her off, motioning for us to be quiet. Irritated, Jules opened her mouth to give him a piece of her mind, but then, she heard it. We all heard it.

The distant sound of a glass door being rattled. Silence. And then footsteps. Hushed male voices.

Someone was here.

Were they looking for us? Did it matter? I was pretty sure no matter who it was, they better not find us here.

"Time to move!" Gawen growled in a low voice. Not low enough though, because one of the people said: "Did you hear that?"

That was all any of us needed. Jules finished stashing the food in her bag and we were running for the back exit, trying to be quiet and not succeeding. Our pursuers were louder, their footsteps pounding through the foyer.

"Quick, go, go, go!" I yelled, yanking open the door and urging my friends through. I was just pulling the heavy steel closed behind me when I realized we had no way of locking it. The bolt was broken, and even if it hadn't been, I didn't have a key. Worse, I caught sight of my brother's face coming across the kitchen.

What could I do?

I remembered the water. The way Reenah had frozen the lock. If only Airmed had taught me how to call up a barrier. If only I'd been born an Earth fae, able to grow plants and make them into prisons. Khai could have melted the door into place.

But I could do none of those things.

"Run!" I yelled.

It was the only thing to do.

My friends needed no prompting, they were already tearing through the alley, outpacing me easily. We needed a place to hide. I was just turning the corner, hitting the sidewalk, when I heard Khai yell my name.

"Ana, wait!" he cried.

Fat chance, I thought. I ran as fast as I could, pushing myself to catch up with my friends as they rounded the block ahead. Suddenly, I was yanked to the side, pulled into an alcove next to a library.

Reenah held a finger to her lips and pulled me down, hiding behind a large book depository. I heard the boys' feet thunder by, and I prayed we'd really lost them. We waited five minutes, and then cautiously made our way back to the street, jogging towards the rail terminal. We'd lost time hiding, meaning we were really cutting it close. If we wanted to make the train, we'd have to be quick.

Every once in a while I would glance back, unable to shake the feeling that we were being followed, but the streets were clear. Hollis and Khai seemed to have lost the trail.

At the station, we paid cash for our tickets and raced for the train, barely making it before the doors slid shut. Chests heaving, we collapsed into a four-square, looking around at each other's flushed, sweaty faces and bursting out laughing.

"We did it!" Jules crowed.

"Yeah, we did," I said, weakly leaning over and giving her a high five."

"Which begs the question, why?" Reenah complained.

"Why what?" I asked, too tired to play around.

"Why did we need to run in the first place? How did they find us?"

"They must have been monitoring the security cams in the streets," Gawen said. "Or they just figured it would be the next place you'd head."

"I guess." I chewed on my lip. I hated feeling like I was that predictable. Plus, I still couldn't stop thinking we hadn't lost them. Had they followed us here, too? I looked around the train, but saw no familiar faces.

Picking up on my emotions, Gawen kicked gently at my foot. "Relax. They're not here. We're good."

"How do you know?"

"I scanned the train when we got on. We're the only fae in this car, and the rest are all families or single riders."

"You can do that?" Jules' eyes bugged out as she twisted in her seat to get a better look at Gawen.

He shrugged, closing his eyes and melting into his seat in that way only the coolest guys can. "Sure. It's a gift."

"I wish I could do that," I said.

"You can. You just need to practice." His eyes were still closed, but he wasn't fooling me. Gawen Black was as alert as ever. "I make it a habit to scan every place I enter, hone my skills."

"Why?" Jules asked.

Reenah snorted. "Gawen likes to pretend he's James Bond."

"I do not," he said, his lips curving up easily. "Why pretend, when you're the real deal?"

We all groaned, Reenah punching him in the shoulder in disgust before settling her own head where she'd punched him.

"Well, I guess we should get some rest. We'll be arriving in less than two hours."

I didn't know about the others, but I was too exhausted to think about how Khai and Hollis had found us. I slipped off my shoes and put my feet up on the seat across from me, nestling them between Reenah and Gawen. I don't remember anything after that, but I must have closed my eyes because I woke to the conductor tapping me on the shoulder.

I looked around. The train had stopped and my friends were fast asleep.

"Time to get up, miss," the conductor said in a deep voice. The car was empty; we were the last ones aboard this part of the train.

"Right, sorry, sir." The sound of my voice woke Jules. I sat up quickly, pulling my feet off Gawen's lap.

"Are we there yet?" Gawen rubbed his eyes.

The conductor was already making his way down the aisle, opening the door to the next compartment.

"Yeah, we're here. The conductor just woke me up. I guess we all missed the announcement."

"Oh my gods, it's so late!" Reenah moaned, checking the time as she stretched.

"I think you mean it's so early," Jules said, yawning.

"That, too," Reenah agreed. "I don't think the subways are even running this early."

"Is there another way to get up to Salem?"

"Without spending beaucoup on a ride? I don't think so." Reenah shook her head slowly, the only speed she seemed able to manage at the moment. "I was here visiting some friends last summer. One time we stayed out dancing all night – we didn't really have any other choice, since the trains shut off from 1 to 5 am."

"Well, we could do that. Go dancing, I mean," Gawen said. Where he got the energy I didn't know. Thankfully, Reenah put the kibosh on that.

"Ugh, no way."

"Tell me about it," Jules commiserated, smoothing her hair away from her forehead and checking the style in the darkened window. "What do you think Ana? What do you want to do? Wait for another train or rent something faster?"

I was tempted to say rent a car, but our funds were limited. Who knew how long it would take to track down the warpers in Salem? We'd need food. Shelter.

Ignoring my own impatience, I suggested we waited for the subways to open. Years ago, Boston's beloved transit system, or "T" had served just a small portion of area towns. One of the first things to happen after the flare was a rapid expansion of all public transport systems. Not only could you get pretty much anywhere in the country via high-speed rail, comfortable buses or subterranean trains, but local transit tended to be free. Even the distance lines were ridiculously cheap: you could ride the system rails across the country for the price of two good books. Yeah, yeah. I tended to measure most goods against the prices of books. Where most girls might price things out against the cost of a new pair of cute boots, I only thought about expanding my library. Shoes might last a season, but books? Books were forever.

Between things like social media, holo-tech and high-speed rails, the world had become a much smaller. Everyone was connected. Third world countries? Developed nations? There was no difference anymore. Everyone played on a level field these days.

Schooling had been expanded to reach 14th grade, and most universities boasted seven-year undergraduate programs. Kids did a lot of studying abroad, internships, and exchanges, making the world even smaller. By the time they graduated, most people had spent significant amounts of time in foreign lands. The idea that people who didn't look like you, act like you, were strangers? That was an outdated nation. Fae, human. Black, white. West, East. We were all one people. One world. It was one of the most amazing cultural shifts in world history, and now, it was at risk.

Knowing about the warpers, I felt like I'd been thrown back in time, into my parents' world. A time where the haves tried to control the have-nots. A world where wars raged beneath the thin veneer or society.

Red-eyed, the four of us trudged down the stairs of the train onto the platform. The conductor watched us disembark, along with the other stragglers. We asked if there was a place we could get an early breakfast and he directed us to the all-night café outside the station. After eating some of the biggest breakfast sandwiches I'd ever seen and dosing ourselves heavily with caffeine, it was time to go.

We walked to the local T station and waited for the first train. The platform filled with a steady stream of cookie-cutter professionals: doctors and nurses; secretaries in sneakers; bankers reading the paper. All waiting for their ride to work. We stuck out like a sore thumb. People our age didn't tend to be early risers.

Not knowing who might be listening to our conversation, we deferred to the commuter silence, remaining mute until we arrived in Salem. I spent most of the ride looking out the window, watching the world rush by. I wasn't going to lie. Everything that had happened so far – the dreams, the running, the emotional scenes that I'd witnessed at the Gregors' headquarters – was taking its toll. The pain I'd felt over and over, the loss and betrayal, they'd hurt. The worst, though, was the hopelessness. Its acid burn was rampaging through me like an infection.

I couldn't help thinking that we would never find him, that my David was gone.

I remembered how his shoulders had sagged, the defeat evident in his posture when he'd been taken away. Even Director Collet had seemed lost, serving up false bravado when he'd said that his friends and husband would find him. If his friends were so powerful, how could they not have found him and the others by now? How could the Light Guard have failed? Had they really not worked together at all? It seemed impossible that they had missed the clues we'd found. Yet, the pen had been there. Untouched. Maybe they'd been too jaded to look harder. Maybe they'd just given up. David had told me the warpers could brainwash most people within a couple weeks, sometimes days. Maybe the starseeds had decided saving their friends was a lost cause. If so, we were on a fool's errand.

When we stepped off the T, out into the bright morning sun of Salem's Atlantic-tinged air, I was lost in thought, wondering what we were doing here.

It was the broken record that I couldn't stop playing in my head. Jules and Reenah were walking ahead and I followed them numbly, not really paying attention to where I was going. An arm circling around my waist scared me, my elbow moving swiftly to jab the interloper.

Gawen grunted in pain but held steady. "Easy Ana, don't hurt me." His voice was low, barely concealing his amusement.

"Sorry. I guess I'm a bit on edge."

"No problem. Though if I was Khai I'd probably just tase you when you weren't expecting it."

"I'm pretty sure he won't ever do that again. I know he regrets having done it. I've made it pretty clear our friendship won't survive any more of that nonsense."

"But didn't you knock him out to escape Valhalla?"

"And?" I ground out.

"Nothing. Just that, maybe, you know, he might consider you guys even now."

"It's not even remotely the same."

"Are you sure?"

"Of course. Don't you see? The outcomes may have been similar, but our reasons were totally different."

"But, wasn't he acting on orders? Trying to keep you safe? Sounds like love to me."

I snorted. "And I suppose I'm selfish because I wanted to be free? Wanted to help someone I love?"

"No, of course not. Simmer down. Anyway, I only wanted to check in with you. I couldn't help seeing how you were feeling. You've got to keep up hope, Ana. I have a feeling we're going to need it."

"My hope?"

"Hope. Faith. Whatever you call it – we're gonna need it."

I mulled his words. Part of me couldn't help being annoyed, feeling like he'd just read my most private thoughts or sneaked a peek in my diary.

"I'm sorry, okay?" He peered down at me and I made a face. "I see people's auras all the time. Reenah thinks I'm nosy, but I can't really help it. It's so hard to turn off, and I feel better, more *me* when just let it flow. I can see that you're hurting Ana. I can see that you're giving up hope. Remember that we're all here for you. We've got all the help and hope you need, okay? If you're feeling lost reach out to us. You don't have to go through this alone."

He gave my waist a small squeeze and dropped his arm. "Okay?"

I sniffled and nodded.

"For better or worse, we're going to find your boy, I promise."

"What if it's too late? What if he's dead? Or worse?" I asked, a shiver running through my body.

Gawen looked at me, his mouth set in a grim smile. The teasing light had gone out of his eyes, but I knew I could trust him to be honest.

"Then at least you'll know."

Chapter 17

Jules and Reenah waited for us at an intersection.

"Where should we go first?" Jules asked when we'd caught up.

"I don't know," I said honestly.

"We could just walk around and see what sticks out," Gawen offered.

Reenah stretched in place, pulling her arms over her head and lunging gracefully to one side. "That seems like a lot of effort for a pretty uncertain payout."

"True," Gawen agreed. "And you know how I feel about wasted effort. What about trolling the Town Hall or the Historical Society? The people there should know all the ins and outs of the town. If the warpers have really been here all these years, then they must have left some sort of a trail."

"I don't know," I said, thinking. "I'm not sure it's a great idea talking to the people there. I mean, the warpers probably have people in charge of all the important places in town: zoning, the historic district, the Chamber of Commerce. I bet they have eyes everywhere."

"Yeah, their headquarters might even be in the town hall." Gawen's fair eyebrows wrinkled with frustration.

"So what are we supposed to do?" Jules' voice lowered as someone passed our little group on the sidewalk. "Stalk the mayor?"

Grim, Reenah spoke up. "That's probably not the best idea. We don't want to show up on their radar before we have a plan."

"Well, then what do we do?" Gawen asked her, sounding irritated.

An idea started to take form in my head. I opened my mouth to speak, then paused, not sure how everybody would react.

"What is it, Ana? Tell us what you're thinking." Jules watched my face. We had always been in sync like that. As different as we were, there'd always been an ability to sense what the other person needed. It had cemented our bond at an early age, keeping us friends over the years despite the fact that we'd joined separate after-school clubs and had polarized views on entertainment.

Encouraged, I blurted out my idea. "What if we go to the library?" Once I'd let out my inner geek, I couldn't help getting excited. "It should have all the old newspapers and the town archives, records of founding families, all sorts of information. I bet we can find some sort of a clue, you know, something to do with the witch trials."

"Right," said Reenah, picking up on my excitement. "If we can figure out who the accused women were having problems with, we should be able to identify the warper families."

"Exactly! We can start before the trials, looked for hints of trouble. If we can see what made those women suspicious of the warpers in the first place, we should be able to trace the warpers through time."

"Through time?" Gawen said. "You mean, to present day?"

"Well, sure. Find the ancestors, find the descendants," I said, feeling hopeful for the first time that day.

"I like it," Reenah said. She'd changed position, standing in tree pose before us with one leg bent so that she reminded me a bit of a flamingo. "It's not a bad idea."

I tucked my hair behind my ears, blushing with pleasure. Jules threw an arm around me and hugged me to her. "Of course it's not a bad idea. It's a brilliant idea! I can always count on Anna to get me to read more."

I caught Gawen looking at my ears.

"You've got elf tips, I never noticed them before."

Did I say I was blushing before? I could feel the right red glow come over, a color I knew would clash badly with my hair, even as I moved my hand to cover my ears. They were a badge of my mixed heritage, though most people didn't care about things like that anymore.

"Don't." Gawen grabbed my hand before I could hide them.

"It's okay. I probably shouldn't have them out anyway, since we're supposed to be incognito and all."

"I suppose," Gawen said, looking sorry. "I didn't mean to make you feel uncomfortable. I think they're cool, actually."

"Yeah, we used to talk about how we wished we had pointy ears, or wings like some of the Ancients," Reenah agreed.

"You think anyone ever will again?" Jules mused.

"Who knows?" Reenah frowned, but she had a gleam in her eye. "It's been a couple thousand years or more since anyone has. But with the flare, I guess anything is possible. Might even be one of you humans who gets a pair first."

"That would be so cool," Jules said, wistful.

"Yeah," I agreed. "But it wouldn't help us now. How about it – library time?"

Everyone voiced their assent, so we found a town map at one of the transit stops and headed to the building, a three-story cube-like structure with a widow's walk on top.

The library didn't open for another couple hours, so we sat down to wait, each of us lost in our thoughts. Finally, an attractive young woman walked by to unlock the doors, smiling at us as we all stood.

"Well, you're all early risers."

"We've been waiting here forever," I muttered under my breath, thinking of how long I'd been wanting to find David. She looked at me oddly but didn't say anything, and I hoped she hadn't heard me. Jules filled in the awkward silence.

"We're here for a research project; we'd love to look through the old town papers."

"Certainly, what dates do you want to see?" The woman held the door for us as we walked inside.

"We'd like to look at the whole year before the Witch Trials," I said.

"Oh well, that could be a problem, since the town's first gazette started circulating in 1768."

"Weren't the trials in the 1600's?" I asked.

The woman nodded. "They started in 1692."

My face fell, diving after my hopes, and she rushed to reassure me.

"But don't worry! We have diaries, town records, letters – all sorts of primary documents you can go through from the years before. Everything has been scanned, of course, since that period is a big draw here." She looked at me more closely. "You look like your ancestors hail from the British Isles. Are you descended from someone here?"

"Oh, no, nothing like that," I said. "We're just doing a project on-" I paused, not sure what to say.

"Possible motivations for the trials, the prior emotional climate of the townspeople," Gawen chimed in, filling the awkward silence. "We're trying to determine what sort of conditions can lead to mass hysteria."

"That sounds really interesting," she said, stepping closer to Gawen. "I think you'll really enjoy going through what our archives. The way people lived back then, don't you find it fascinating? Imagine, no running water, no modern conveniences." She shivered delicately. "And the work to feed yourself through the winter months-"

"Sometimes, I'm not sure I want to live this far north, even with all the amenities. Without them? I would have been on the first wagon the south," Jules laughed.

The woman led us over to a large communal holo-desk, the glass-topped table gleaming.

"This should have everything you want. If you need any help at all, just let me know. A generous donation allowed us to finish digitizing everything a few years ago, so at least you won't have to worry about wading through miles and miles of microfiche."

Reenah wrinkled her nose, while Gawen and Jules looked equally mystified. I'd spent enough time in older libraries to know exactly what the woman was talking about. The long film made up of individual slides had allowed researchers to scroll picture-by-picture, rather than handling the actual original documents. The technology had been older than my parents, but it worked. The internet had pushed a lot of schools to digitize their libraries early, but many smaller facilities had lagged behind, lacking both funds and savvy personnel. We were lucky, and the librarian said as much.

"Before, your search could have taken days. Now, because of our transition to holo-tech, every file will have been assigned meta-data. Our state-of-the-art AI system will be able to combine the data with your searches to target your needs quite swiftly."

If they were using the newest tech, we might be done in less than an hour. Even the slowest holo-desks were using AI processors driven by the metallic Aura Quartz technology Simon Lasky had discovered in 2028, making searches even more intuitive. It seemed they got smarter and faster every year. If only we knew exactly what we were looking for.

The librarian smiled at us. "I imagine you'll find more than you need for your paper." Her eyes lingered on Gawen, who smiled back appreciatively.

"Thanks for taking the time to explain that to us," he said. Now it was the librarian's turn to blush.

"Anytime. My name is Sarah, I'll be around shelving last night's returns if you need anything." She turned and walked away, definitely adding some extra swing to her hips.

"Woo," Rihanna crooned, reaching under Gawen's arm to tickle him. "Looks like somebody's got an admirer."

Gawen fiddled with his hair, half of which had fallen out the bun on top of his head, and tucked the errant strands behind both ears. "Come on let's see what we can find." He seemed determined to ignore her insinuation.

The four of us took our seats in silence. The others took chairs at the sides of the desk, giving me the center console. I had a feeling it was more about their lack of familiarity with the library research system than any edge they thought I might have. Quickly I input our search parameters, gliding my hands over the smooth glass and tapping efficient commands. I called up four strands of information trails, one for each of us to read through, using a sweeping motion to push the holograms over to each of them and give them access to the meta-data functions.

"Alright, everybody start reading," I instructed. Everyone started scrolling through their feeds and we worked quietly.

Two hours later we were still at it, my friends' eyes glazing over. Even I had started to fall prey to a feeling of boredom.

"This is ridiculous. We should take a break, maybe walk through town and see if we get any lightning bolts of inspiration or whatever. We can come back with fresh eyes, at least."

"Don't give up hope. We're going to crack this," Gawen said, bumping shoulders with me.

"I know. I'm just frustrated, that's all."

"I know, me too. Let's do this for ten more minutes, then we can go find some lunch."

"Lunch?" I looked at the clock on my screen. We were barely even in brunch territory. "Do you ever stop eating?"

"No, he does not," Reenah murmured, eyes glued to her screen.

I followed their lead and went back to speed-reading the feed, words and pictures scrolling by in a blur. I could tell my mind was starting to wear out; there was only so long my eyes and brain could accommodate the tedium. It might not have been lunchtime yet, but some caffeine was definitely in order. But if they could do it, these people who barely knew me, and didn't know David at all, well then so could I.

I must have zoned out, because the next thing I knew a raven was cawing in my face, brushing my nose with its wings as it flew past.

My eyes followed the flight of the bird, tracking it as it navigated the spaces between trees. This time, we were in the woods but the trees were spaced out, the ground manicured, as if someone was planning a park. You could tell that this place had been touched by human hands, though it still felt vaguely wild and forbidden.

The bird cawed, reminding me to pay attention. I took off, jogging after him, tracking desperately to track the birds' erratic flight. When it finally stopped, I realized that once again it had led me to the ancient oak.

What was the message?

This time, the door among the roots stood propped open, as if in invitation. Was this David's doing? Was he trying to reach out to me? I took a step forward, and paused. What if it was a trap? I had so little experience with starseeds, even less with warpers. Could they enter my mind through a dream, mind-warp me, control my thoughts? I hesitated, my hand on the door.

Suddenly, a loud beeping noise sounded nearby. The door faded away and my elbow bumped against the table where I'd been resting it, supporting my head as I daydreamed. I tried to rub the pain away, scanning the room. Someone had tried to walk through the exit without checking out their books. A stern-faced librarian crooked her finger, beckoning the offender over to the circulation desk.

Gawen looked over at me, chuckling.

"Falling asleep on the job?"

"I was dreaming," I said slowly, still cradling my elbow.

"You know we can't be anything but friends, right? You really shouldn't be thinking about me that way."

I glanced up, startled. "What? No, I didn't do that, I wouldn't-"

"I'm just joking," he said. "Relax."

"Oh," I breathed.

"So what did you dream about?" Jules sounded concerned.

"It was the same dream I've had before. I was in the woods, a raven led me to that old oak tree."

"You don't think it's some sort of a clue, do you? Like maybe there's a big giant oak tree in the woods that we should be looking for instead of scrolling through holo-files?" Jules sounded hopeful. Research really wasn't her thing.

"I don't know. I mean it's really way out in the middle of the woods. I don't see how someone would have the sort of technology to hide the entrance to a whole facility like that in a tree. Not to mention how inconvenient the whole thing would be."

"They've hidden in the woods before," Jules reminded me.

"True. But then what's the deal with the raven? He is super persistent, let me tell you. Do you think it's David somehow?"

"I don't know," Jules wondered. "Maybe we should do a search for ravens and old oaks."

"Sounds like you guys should check out Burying Point Cemetery." Sarah was walking by and joined our conversation. "Sorry, I wasn't trying to eavesdrop, but I heard something about the old oak."

"Um, yeah," Reenah drawled, like she was pretty sure Sarah had meant to do just that. "We found some papers talking about a raven and an oak tree, maybe one that had fallen down, like a really big old tree? Does that mean anything to you?"

"Well of course. Everybody knows the old oak." We looked at her, astonished. She rushed to explain. "It's at the center of Burying Point, the oldest graveyard in Salem. There's a memorial for the hangings nearby, you should check it out. Anyhow, tourists love to come and take rubbings of the gravestones, see who they might have been related to, you know that kind of thing." She explained this with a roll of her eyes, as if she thought the whole idea was kind of silly.

"So you're saying the old oak is in the middle of a graveyard, not woods?" I asked.

"Well, I'm sure it was a forest at some point, everything was when they first settled here."

I thought back to what Phineas had said about the warpers settling Salem. If that was true maybe the old oak marked an important place for them. While I was thinking, the librarian had kept talking and I struggled to shake myself out my thoughts. She caught my attention fully when I heard her say something about a raven.

"I'm sorry could you repeat what you just said? I was sort of spacing out for a second."

"I was telling your friends about The Raven's Grimoire. It's a great little shop. The building's been in the same family for almost as long as the town's been around. It's been a lot of different things over the year – boarding house, offices, hat shop. The Grim is awesome though, a really cute little shop. People swear by the owner's love spells."

"I bet they do," I whispered, mind racing. If the owner was a warper, a bard like Elaine, then I imagined that their love spells would be extremely effective. All she had to do was tell someone that her spell had worked and they would believe it was true. Talk about easy money. It was the ultimate con.

My friends and I eyed each other and came to silent agreement.

"What's the best way to get there?"

"The cemetery's pretty close to here. Just take a left when you get outside and follow Essex Street, turn right on Washington, and then left again on Front Street. From there, just follow the signs, you can't miss it."

"Thanks for your help," Gawen said, standing and shaking her hand.

Sarah struggled to maintain a professional manner, failing miserably. "Of course, it's what I'm here for. If you have any other questions just let me know. I better get back to shelving or Mrs. Conway over there's going to have my hide." She nodded over towards the older woman manning the front desk.

Gawen shuddered theatrically. "Yeah, she looks mean, I wouldn't want to cross her. You better go."

Somehow, he managed to dismiss her in a way that sounded like he would rather have her stay. She looked up at him and flushed, the red starting at her chest and quickly creeping up her neck, all the way to the roots of her hair. Quickly, she smiled and hurried away.

Hefting my bag up onto my shoulder to leave, I wondered idly if that was what I looked like when I blushed. As a natural redhead, embarrassment had always been my nemesis.

Chapter 18

The Grim looked like any other old house in Salem. White wood siding, dark shutters, and fancy carved banisters along the front porch. It was large, with the shop below and what seemed to be curtained living quarters above.

The storefront itself wasn't as creepy as I'd expected. A hand-painted raven on the sign held a knobby wand in its beak, showering sparks over the words "Grimoire". The largest sparkles dotted the I's. Wide plate-glass windows were filled with herbs in jars, handmade besoms and a large mock-parchment scroll carved out of plywood. Red paint masqueraded as blood, detailing the ingredients of a love spell. At least, I hoped it was blood.

"Rose petals, two hairs from a white cat, frankincense, light of a full moon, a nightingale's song." Jules read the spell, skepticism ripe in her voice.

"They've done everything to make this look like it's the real deal," Reenah said.

"Maybe it is," I said, hoping the opposite.

Gawen shook his head. "This place is angry. It's like the Gregors' headquarters, alive, except it almost likes being dark."

"Is that possible? I thought buildings were made to protect people. Are you telling me that a building can actually become twisted and take on the evil of its inhabitants?" I asked.

Gawen shrugged. "Poltergeists used to be a lot more common when there were more dark deeds going on in the world. Most of the time paranormal activity could be traced to latent fae bloodlines being stirred up with hormones or anxiety, but my dad says sometimes it was the buildings themselves. Taking on impressions, becoming infected by negativity. They can be healed and rebalanced, but it takes conscious work and people need to know what they are doing."

"So if this building has been in a warper family for many generations, the building could have bonded with them?" I asked, slightly horrified.

"More or less," Gawen said.

"But what about the land?" Jules asked. Wouldn't the earth be angry to be used like this? I mean, what about Mother Nature's revenge and all that?"

"Land doesn't much care either way – unless something really terrible happens that it might hold an imprint of. I guess you can say the land believes in co-creation. Free will. How someone chooses to use it, that's their problem. At the core, the land can't really ever be changed. Do you know why?" Gawen looked at me and I flashed back to Earth Science 101. Science tended to give me panic attacks, but I thought I had an inkling of what he was talking about.

"Its core. That's Anansanna, right?" I ventured.

"Right." Gawen beamed at me and I felt like I had passed a test. "Nothing can change that. It would take a massive, horrific cataclysm to shut down Anansanna. It's almost impossible, and not worth even thinking about."

"Why not?" Jules asked.

"Because," Reenah answered glumly, "the whole planet would be dead then. Anansanna is part of everything. It's what fuels the photonic replication of our cells. Without it, the land would die; people, animals, plants, everything. It might take days or months, but in the end everything would cease to matter. Literally."

I'd barely passed Cellular Biology, but I got the gist of what she was saying. It was a ghastly scenario that didn't bear thinking about, Gawen was right.

"So what do we do now?" The hours posted in the window stated that they were open for business. I saw someone inside walking around and wondered if they'd noticed us staring at the house. "It's probably not smart for us all to go in, just in case something happens."

"I'll bite." Reenah shivered. "This place gives me the creeps. I'll check out the cemetery while you-"

The front door opened, a shop bell tinkling within. Silvery hair gleamed in the sun as a woman poked her head outside.

"In the market for some spells?" The smile on the woman's face was bright and sincere but my stomach lurched in fear. I looked at Gawen trying to hide the shock on my face. The Grim's spell-caster wasn't a speaker like Elaine. She *was* Elaine. "Come on, come on everybody. I'm running a special today on tarot readings. You get four for the price of three. That's it, don't be shy. I promise not to tell you you're going to die or anything terrible like that."

Elaine chuckled at her lame joke. Reenah shrugged and led the rest of us up the stairs, probably not wanting to offend Elaine. I didn't feel like we'd been commanded to enter, but I wasn't sure we would know if we had. Marching after Gawen, I connected to Anansanna, putting up psychic shields and trying to bolster my aura. I didn't know if it would deter the woman's bardic power, but it couldn't hurt. I hoped that Gawen was doing the same. As we entered, I realized that Jules and Reenah hadn't actually seen the visions we'd experienced in Montreal. They had no idea that this woman was Elaine Carhartt. Gawen and I would have to shield all of us. Had my dreams been David reaching out to me, trying to draw me in, or something else?

So much here was unknown. We needed to regroup, but we didn't get a chance. Before we could form any kind of a plan the woman was asking which one of us would go first and Jules cracked a joke about being the sacrificial sheep as she disappeared from view, following Elaine into a curtained alcove. After some furious whispering, we decided to split up and look around.

Nonchalantly, I wandered through the room to the left. I picked up small dragons, pretending to look at their prices, and tested the edges on golden athames for sharpness while my eyes sought anything that might scream "Starseeds hidden here." Gawen called my name in a low voice and I put down the red crystal I'd been gazing at, rushing to join him.

"Did you find something?"

Standing in a hallway, Gawen motioned silently to a security camera monitoring a closed door marked "Private." It could have been an office, a closet, a basement, anything. But one thing was clear – it was off-limits.

My spidey senses were tingling. I wanted inside that room.

"What about the camera?" I asked softly. "We can't just waltz in."

"We could always say we thought it was the bathroom," Gawen suggested.

Reenah snorted. "Please. Even you can't pull off looking that clueless. Let me take care of it."

Reenah pursed her lips and blew gently towards the camera. Its glass lens fogged over and she nudged me forward.

"Go. I'll tell them that you were bored and wanted to check out the cemetery."

"Okay," Gawen nodded. "But be careful. That woman in there? That's Elaine, the warper who cleared out the Montreal headquarters."

Reenah blanched, folding her lips into a line. Quickly, she hugged Gawen, then urged us towards the door.

We snuck forward, quietly opening the door and slipping inside. Gawen reached out, pulling a string to illuminate a cramped wooden landing at the top of some stairs. The walls were old and could have used a fresh coat of paint, but the stairs had been rebuilt with thick, heavy-duty treads.

Behind us, I could hear the bell over the front entrance to the shop jingle. I stiffened, worried we might be about to have some company.

"Reenah's crafty," Gawen whispered down at me. "She's making it sound like we left."

"Do you think she'll be okay?"

"Sure," Gawen said, forcing confidence into his voice. "The warpers are worried about starseeds, not a few random fae teenagers."

"I hope you're right."

We ventured down the stairs. The unfinished basement looked well over a hundred years old, its walls made of stone, the floor concrete. An ancient oil furnace sat unused in one corner next to the building's water heater and a first generation zero-emission Tesla heater. As big as the space was, I realized the proportions seemed off compared to the outer footprint of the house. I didn't see any crawl spaces, like there would usually be in a colonial basement. I turned the corner around the stairs. Several sets of shelves leaned against the wall, holding cans of paint, odds and ends.

"I don't get it. Why train a camera on the basement if there's nothing down here other than an old boiler? It doesn't add up." Gawen bent to look under the empty oil tank.

I didn't answer, just stood there staring at the shelves. Something was off, I knew it. But what?

Frustrated, I kicked at the floor. That's when my eyes registered what my brain must have already picked up. Scuff marks in grit and dust.

"This shelf has been moved! Over here," I pointed to the shelves on the left and we tried to pull them away from the wall. Nothing. They wouldn't budge.

"Who keeps this many empty paint cans, anyway," I grumbled. I tried to move some of the cans but I couldn't; they were fixed to the shelf. Turning my head to look around, I saw that one side of the shelf had hinges. The hardware had been painted to blend in with the raw stone walls, but once you saw it they were obvious. "This is some kind of a secret door, look! We need to figure out how to open it."

Again, I tried moving the canisters, figuring maybe one would act as a lever, emulating a secret book in an old mystery novel. Nothing happened.

"Hold on, I think I got something." Gawen pointed at a red light switch that said "Emergency Shut-Off."

"Yeah, so?"

"That's for turning off the old boiler, right? Why would they have a switch for the boiler here when there's already one there, next to the stairs? Those Tesla heating cores have their own automatic safety features, so it wouldn't be for that, see?"

I looked. There were two emergency shut off switches. One's wires ran across the ceiling to the oil furnace, but the other one ran over my head, towards the shelves. Gawen flipped the switch and the shelf swung open to reveal a recessed door behind the stone façade.

The hallway on the other side was just like the one in my dream. Sterile white walls. Fluorescent lights. We entered, and the door swung shut behind us. Gawen didn't hesitate. He started trying each door, looking for answers.

"Don't bother. If it's like my dream, David's not in these. Besides, I doubt even the warpers would be so cocky as to keep their prisoners right by the entrance."

"Well, they're cocky enough not to have guards posted."

Uneasy, I looked for hidden cameras in the hall but saw none. Gawen was right. Hopefully, they had skimped on security in other areas, too.

We continued down the hall, finally coming to a set of double doors. Rather than being at the end of the hall, as in my dream, these were set into an alcove. Otherwise, they looked the same.

"This is it. I found David through here," I whispered.

We pushed our way through the doors, entering a large nursing ward with multiple beds. The faint smell of chemicals and death made me want to gag. Like in my dream, there was a nurse, except this one wasn't friendly. Seeing us, she startled and dropped her silver tray of needles. She took a deep breath like she was getting ready to cry out. Gawen threw up his hands before she could do anything, blue light flashing from his hands. Knocked back, she landed on the floor unconscious. I started to congratulate Gawen for his quick thinking when my eyes fell on David.

As before, he was unconscious, hooked up to several IVs containing an unknown cocktail of warper drugs. I rushed over, cupping his face in my palm. Weeks of beard growth ticked my skin.

"David! Oh, David. Wake up, honey, wake up." When he didn't, I focused my gaze on his arms. Needles pierced this vulnerable skin at both wrists. I reached for one arm and Gawen stopped me.

"Wait. We don't know what's in these. What if it's all that's keeping him alive?"

"Nothing the warpers are doing to him could possibly be good. Besides, we can't exactly bring the IVs with us."

Gawen pressed his lips together but didn't argue. Grimly, I eased the needles out of David's arms one by one, letting the leads fall and drip onto the floor. Gawen looked over the five IV bags hanging by the bed.

"I don't know what any of this means," he said. "A couple of them aren't even properly labeled. Like this one, it just says Q32."

"So you're saying we don't know what's in it?"

He shook his head, taking a picture of each bag with his chat.

I turned back to David, thinking about how I'd woken him up in my dream. Would it work in real life? There was only one way to find out. I leaned over and held David's wan face in my hands, kissed him softly.

"You need to wake up, David." I moved my hands to David's chest and started to pour healing energy into him.

I focused on everything I could think of that was vibrant and alive. I imagined the light of Anansanna flowing up through my feet into his body. "You can do this David I know you can." I kept whispering encouraging words while Gawen watched silently at my side. After a moment, he stepped away, checking on the other patients and removing their IVs. When he'd finished, he came back to the bed next to David's and held his hands over the occupant. One hand over the young girl's forehead, another at her abdomen, he looked up at me, no smile on his usually cheery face.

"I can't heal her like you can, but I figured maybe I could scan them and see what's going on." His lips twisted into a grimace. "I'm not getting anything from her. No fear, nothing. She feels dead inside."

"No, not dead," I said, thinking out loud. "She might be a traveler, like David. She could be astral traveling, then she'd feel empty, like you say."

"Isn't she too young for that? I mean, didn't you say the starseeds' powers activate in their late twenties?"

"You're right. She doesn't look like she's even in high school yet." I sighed.

Gawen looked down at the girl in front of him. "But maybe, I don't know, maybe that's just it."

"What do you mean?"

"Well, trying to activate powers in a starseed before the normal awakening, that sounds like something they'd love to do. It would give their foot soldiers an edge, you know, while they're still young and strong. I don't know. I don't know anything. Honestly, I'm feeling a little out of my depth here, Ana." Gawen tried to smile and failed.

"Me, too. You've given me an idea though. Maybe it's not David's body I should be healing. Maybe I just need to push the healing deeper, past David's cells to his emotions."

"If that's the case, then maybe I can do something over here, too," Gawen said, looking hopeful. He closed his eyes and concentrated, and I did the same.

I could feel myself starting to get tired, emotions overtaking me. Fear. Despair. If I couldn't heal him, we would have to carry him out of here.

I was just about to say that when I felt David's chest lift, a rattled groan rising from within. I lifted my hands and then thought better of it, replacing them on his chest.

"Wake up, David. Can you hear me?"

He moaned again, but didn't open his eyes. I looked at Gawen, who was watching us but still stood over the young girl.

"I need your help," I said.

"What can I do?" he asked, moving to the other side of David's bed.

"Put your hands on mine and just, I don't know, send love or something. He needs more energy than I can pull but maybe with the two of us..."

"Okay." Gawen closed his eyes and I felt the positive feelings pouring through me.

The despair lifted and I felt my connection to Anansanna return, a surge of red sparkles rising up my legs towards David. I felt like I was floating, rising on the heat of the sun. It wasn't painful but my whole body warmed intensely as the energy surged through me. I felt the muscles in his arm twitch under my hand and I focused on that spot, sending more and more energy into him.

"Come on, David," I murmured "Wake up!"

He grunted in protest, his head moving to one side.

"That's it, David." I focused all my concentration and love on him. After what felt like an eternity, but was probably only thirty seconds, his eyes opened. The warm chocolate orbs stared blankly, black pupils shrinking and dilating repeatedly as they tried to adjust to the light.

"Water," he rasped, licking his lips.

Gawen filled a small paper cup and handed it to me. Gently Gawen lifted his head so he could drink, and I held the cup to David's lips while his eyes remained locked on mine. Finally, he pushed away the empty cup and fell back on his pillow.

"Ana, is it really you? If this is another trick—"

"It's not a trick, I swear. It's me."

"You've tricked me before," he said, turning his head to the side.

Pain twisted through my gut at what he'd been through. I thought for a moment, trying to think of something I could say that would prove I was really me, and not some warper imposter. I chewed my lip discarding memories even as they came. Then, I had it.

"The second time you saw my brother, he strung you up with vines from trees and Khai tased you."

"Ana?"

"Yes, it's me!"

David shook his head, lips puckered as if he was tasting something foul and bitter. "No. You've all been in my head. You know everything about me. You could know that, too."

"David, it's me, I promise. You don't know what I've been through to get here, and I'm sorry it's taken me so

173

long, but I've come to get you out of here." I kissed him on the lips and sent more healing energy into him. "That's me, healing you. Warpers can't do that."

"Heck, most fae can't do it," Gawen muttered, sounding jealous.

"That's right," I grinned, never taking my eyes off David's. "Just me."

"Ana, it's really you?" He sounded like a little boy meeting Santa in the living room on Christmas Eve, and the hope in his voice just about killed me.

"Yes, David, it's me. Now come on, we've got to get you out of here." I helped him up, and he looked around the room.

"How are we going to wake up all these people?" he asked.

"I don't think we can," I said. "We've tried, but it took everything we had just to get you to open your eyes."

"It was close, man, we almost couldn't do it. I don't think we have time to try on anyone else."

Somehow, Gawen's words galvanized me. "No, David's right. We have to try."

I walked over to the next bed and put my hands several inches above the sleeping man's chest, probing his energy. I could sense he dozed even more deeply than David. Gawen looked at the IVs nearby.

"He was on something different." He moved to another bed. "This one, too. They're all different,"

"They were experimenting," David said, trying to sit up. His breath came in short, shallow gasps.

"I'm starting to get a bad feeling about this. Something doesn't feel right," Gawen said quietly. "I think we should go get help."

"Why would you want to do that?" a familiar voice asked from behind me. Phineas, the man who had taken Cliff Collet at gunpoint, stood at the door with crossed arms and a small army of muscled fighters at his back.

Chapter 19

He gazed at me hungrily, making me think of some kind of deranged cheetah.

"Hello, Ana. What a pleasure to see you again."

David looked at me quizzically. "Again?"

"Phineas has been using your astral dreams to connect with me," I explained. David blanched, his face taking on a blue cast as it lost the little bit of color it had started with.

"You know my name, young Ana. I don't recall telling you my name before."

"No, you didn't." I had no interest in engaging in any small talk with the grease ball. Phineas narrowed his eyes and gave a small flick of his head. Several men moved forward to take us by the arms while the armed guards on either side of him kept their guns trained on us. I didn't really want to take any chances that my shields worked against bullets, but I knew I had to do something before anyone else showed up. I gathered up all my power, expanding my aura, imagining how it would knock the people holding me backward, but nothing happened.

Well, barely anything. The barest of glows emanated from my arms and the men stumbled a bit, but they did not release my arms. Had I used up all my power healing David? Was such a thing even possible? I looked at Gawen and he stared back at me, giving a small shake of his head. Whatever was going on was affecting him, too.

Phineas cackled. It was as annoying in real life as it had been in my dreams and visions. Annoying, and eminently disturbing.

"What's so funny?" I ground out.

"This entire facility is lined with six inches of melted Popigai meteorite from Siberia. It took years of experimenting but eventually we found something that cuts you off from your red sun, diminishing your fae powers."

"But you can't do that. Without Anansanna, earth-based life will die. You'd be harming yourselves, too," Gawen said, shocked.

"You'd think so, wouldn't you? But it turns out that our Nommo DNA makes us even less human than we originally realized. Without Anansanna pumping her idiotic ions into our blood, we grow stronger while the rest of you, fae and humans alike, grow weak and age faster. You should see the fae we've had here for the last ten years. They have no powers, their hair is grey, they even have wrinkles. It's depressing actually – for them!"

He started laughing again and the men holding me chuckled along with him. Gawen's eyes widened, horrified, and we both renewed our struggles against our captors. My face reddened with effort but the guards remained immovable. Phineas looked bored, like he was waiting for a child to finish having a temper tantrum.

"Please, young ones. Don't bother. I will give you the same offer we give everyone of your kind. You can join us or you can die a slow, human death."

"Why? Why would you do this to us? To anyone? What is your problem?" I demanded.

"My problem? My problem is that just when things were starting to get good for us, you fae had to come along and change the world, give humans an edge. Pretty soon, they'll be just like you."

"So?"

"Come on. The writing's on the wall. In a hundred years, starseeds will be the new slave caste. We won't be able to hide anymore. Starseeds will be the only ones dying from normal lifespans, outmatched by your ridiculous elemental powers. We are the ones who were supposed to inherit the earth and you ruined it," he snarled.

Gawen snorted. "You're kidding, right? We built this earth. We made this planet. You guys," he snarled, "you're just interlopers. Crossbreeds that don't belong here. The Nommo knew it. They saw how you guys turned out and they left, horrified. They abandoned you. If anyone deserves to inherit the planet trust me, it's not you."

I snickered. "Yeah, it's like when you break up with your totally crazy boyfriend, so to placate him you say 'It's not you, it's me.' Except in this case it was your parents, the Nommo, who dumped you and they had no problem saying 'It's not us, it's you.'"

David giggled, a crazy sound tripping out of his mouth like he couldn't believe I'd just egged on Phineas. Phineas glared at him and he slapped a hand over his mouth, terror creeping into his eyes. *What else had Phineas done to him?*

"Take them away, all three of them. Put them in Quadrant C where they can watch each other age for the next few decades. By the time they start getting grey hairs, they should be willing to cooperate."

Gawen and I fought as they dragged us out into the hall, but it didn't make a difference. The men holding us were like mountains. The one holding David grinned at me.

"Maybe we should just knock them out. It would make it easier to have fun when we get down to QC, don't you think?" he suggested, raising an eyebrow and leering at me. Bile rose in my throat at the thought of that man with his hands on me and not being able to fight back.

"You wouldn't dare," shouted David.

"I'll do what I want," the guy said, cuffing him on the ear, knocking David to the floor. He fumbled weakly, unable to get up. Weeks in their hospital of horrors had obviously taken their toll.

"It's okay, David," I said, trying to keep my voice from wavering. "We're going to get out of this. We'll figure it out, I promise."

The men laughed and one of them patted me on the head as if I was a cute dog who'd just entertained them with some tricks.

"Oh, honey. You're not going anywhere, trust me," the man on my left said quietly in my ear, satisfaction rich in his voice. "Although I can get you some better accommodations, if you decide you want to cooperate."

His eyes ran up and down the length of my body, leaving no doubt as to what he meant. A growl rose up in my throat and I reached for the power of Anansanna with all my might. She felt so distant, the torrent of sparkles that I'd called up before now felt like dust on the wind, fragile and sparse. What I wouldn't have given in that moment for some of Airmed's gladiolus essence.

One of the men yanked David back to his feet and we all started off down the hall again: Gawen and I resisting as much as we could, David's head hung low in defeat. One of the men had just called the elevator when the sound of pounding feet made me turn and look over my shoulder.

I didn't even get a chance to say my brother's name before white-hot streaks of lightning sparked along the hallway. The beams splintered in several directions, tasing each of the seven guards at once. My arms tingled from the indirect electrocution, but I weathered the storm. Without anyone to hold him up, David fell to the floor again, his legs giving way underneath in him. Khai and Hollis didn't slow down, thundering towards us. As he ran, my brother called on the earth, thorny vines cracking through the ceiling and walls, growing down at record speed to cover the men's arms and legs in twisting gnarls. Unless one of the men was carrying an ax, they were going to have a hard time freeing themselves.

I looked at Hollis and Khai in wonder. I'd never been so happy to see my brother in my entire life and all the anger I'd felt towards Khai evaporated in an instant.

"How did you find us?" I asked, breathless.

"We've been following you since Montreal." My brother grasped my arms and looked down at me, examining me from head to toe. "We can talk later. Now, we need to move."

Gawen reached down to help David up and my brother helped him, the two of them working as a team to drag David's limp body between them towards the exit. I stared after them and paused, looking up into Khai's eyes. The fluorescent lighting reflected strangely in them, making them look like they'd been infused with neon flash.

"There are so many people here. Not just starseeds, but fae, too. We have to help them."

"We do, but not today, Ana. Right now, we've got to get out of here."

Remembering how drained my powers had become in the short time I'd been here, I knew Khai was right. The longer we stayed the weaker we'd become. But the warpers wouldn't stay here now that we'd found them. They'd move again. What if we lost them, for good? I wanted to discuss it more, but Hollis and Gawen had already left through the door at the end of the hall, heading back to the Grim.

Khai laid a gentle hand on my back. "We'll come back. We'll save everyone, I promise. But please, Ana, right now we really have to go."

A bell dinged behind us and I turned to see the elevator open. Several men got out, looked at the vines covering the hall, their guards on the floor, and sprang into action. In an instant, Khai and I were fighting for our lives. Every ounce of training we'd ever had was put to use. I could tell that Khai tried to harness his fire abilities several times, but his power was waning already. I jabbed my attacker in the throat with my elbow, sending him to his knees gasping, and aimed a roundhouse kick at his head. He fell back, unconscious. The rest of the guards were on Khai, covering him like ants on candy, having deemed me of little threat. Against their towering mass and number, I supposed I was.

"Run, Ana, run! Get out of here," Khai shouted.

"I can't leave you!" I cried. I started towards the melee, trying to decide which guard to go for first.

"Please, Ana, run. I can't live with myself if something happens to you. Please, just go!" His eyes watered and I knew it wasn't just from the pain the guards were inflicting on him. Staring into his eyes, I felt everything he was feeling, the full depth of his fear that something would happen to me. Just thinking about me in danger made him crazy, like he was dying on the inside. Everything he'd ever done had come from a place of love, and not the brotherly kind.

I took a step backwards, reeling from his emotions. I wasn't sure he even knew what he was feeling.

His eyes pled with me, urged me to flee. One of the guards turned towards me, as if suddenly realizing that maybe he needed to pay attention. The man's face turned into a mask of rage at the sight of me, and I realized I knew him. Riley Cougan, the warper I'd left on the Long Trail with a broken leg.

"Ana, run! Get help." Khai's voice came out ragged as he took another punch to the gut. I looked behind me. Hollis and Gawen had already gone upstairs; they had no idea what we were facing.

"That's right, run, Tinkerbell," Cougan sneered. Cougan pulled a gun from his belt and aimed at me. Even at their best, I wasn't sure that my shields could turn back bullets. Khai was right. I needed help. I turned and sprinted down the hallway. I was small, but I had always been fast. Cougan's feet pounded down the hall after me as he called for me to stop.

I didn't listen.

A shot rang out, the sound deafening in the stark corridor, and I felt a searing pain in my calf. It hurt, but I was pretty sure getting caught by Cougan would hurt worse. I ran faster. Just as I put my hand on the door, an alarm sounded, a monotone voice announcing imminent lockdown procedures.

I yanked on the door but paused, looking behind me. Cougan was still several yards away, a noticeable limp slowing him down. I watched Khai being dragged into the elevator, my ribs aching like every single one of them was cracking from the inside out, the side of my leg on fire.

"Khai!" I yelled.

If he answered, I was too far away to hear him. My pursuer was just feet away now. I jumped through the door and pulled it shut, the lock sliding automatically home with an audible click.

On the other side, I could hear Cougan pounding on the door and swearing. I wanted to turn and tear down the door myself. Lucky for me, it wouldn't open again, not with the lockdown being enforced. I was safe, but I wasn't relieved.

What the hell had just happened?

Chapter 20

The lockdown alarm was fainter in the basement, competing with the high-pitched blare of a fire-alarm upstairs. I doubted anyone upstairs had even heard the gunshot. Quickly, I flipped the burner switch and the shelves swung shut behind me, hiding the inner door once more.

I needed to think. The noise was making it impossible. My heart raced, but that didn't explain the pain I was experiencing in my chest. Had I just lost Khai forever? I knew I shouldn't think that way, but I felt like I was dying inside.

"Ana, Khai, move it!" Hollis' deep voice reverberated through the basement as he yelled down the stairs. I had to keep moving. Every step counted now, every minute.

We'd only seen a portion of the warpers' facility, and it had been huge. From what I could tell, there were other floors and sectors, most definitely ranging under multiple properties. There would be other exits. Even now, they were probably figuring out a way to override the lockdown so they could evacuate the prisoners, moving them somewhere else. Like cockroaches, they would know how to hide.

I ran up the stairs and saw Elaine lying on the floor and looked at Hollis.

"Is she-?"

"Asleep," he shouted over the alarm. "I knocked her out when we came upstairs, but not before she was able to set off the panic button."

He pointed at a red light switch by the basement door, again marked "Emergency Shutoff." Gawen was supporting David, who seemed to be standing better now. The adrenaline was probably doing wonders for him, but it wouldn't last forever.

"We've got to get out of here. They'll be coming for us. I assume you have a car or something?" I asked Hollis.

"Yeah, we brought a van. Where's Khai?"

I ignored him and started going through kitchen drawers. I tossed him a roll of duct tape.

"Tie her up. Make sure you cover her mouth, otherwise she can make you do things..."

"Ana," Hollis demanded, not moving.

"He's not coming, okay? They took him, Hollis. He told me to run and I did and they took him. Dammit!" I kicked the basement door. "Is that what you want to hear? They took him, and there's nothing we can do about it. Not now. But Elaine? She can help us. She's going to help us get him back. By the gods, I swear she will."

Hollis looked at me, stunned. He opened his mouth to speak, then clamped his jaw closed. Ever-capable, he launched himself into action, trussing Elaine up like a Christmas roast and hefting her over his shoulder. Without another word, he turned and left.

Gawen followed with David and I brought up the rear. As we walked through the shop, I grabbed a pair of golden athames, sharp double-sided daggers that looked nicely weighted. Perfect for throwing, or maybe just putting the fear of the gods into Elaine.

I imagined she thought the fae were weak. Harmless elven folk, light-hearted and mild tempered.

She hadn't met me. Elaine was going to wish she'd never messed with the fae, never taken David, never joined the warpers. "She's going to pay," I vowed under my breath, climbing into the van next to David in the back. Putting my arm around him and pulling him to me, I wasn't sure who was comforting whom.

I flinched as Hollis slammed the back doors closed on Elaine. Jules turned and looked at me from the front seat.

"Your leg! Ana, you're bleeding." Then her eyes widened. "Where's Khai?"

I gave my head a tiny shake and fingered the gash in my pants. It was wet with blood where the bullet had seared my skin as it winged me. Unable to meet Jules' eyes, I looked out the window, absently stroking David's hair. He'd slumped against me and I could feel his heart rate slowing, exhaustion taking over his body. Here, outside of the warpers' lair, I could feel my power returning. What good was it to me? I didn't need it now. *Too late*, I thought, and fed it into David instead, like a balm for his mind and soul. In seconds, he was snoring gently on my shoulder.

"Hollis?" Jules said in a small voice. "What happened in there?"

"I don't know."

His silver eyes met mine in the mirror. Where Mom's were always warm, his stung like ice.

"But we're gonna find out."

Characters & Terms
A Fae & Starseed Compendium

Aeden – The land of the fae within the earth, the origin of all Eden myths and Hollow Earth theories. The word means gifts of fire.

Aho-em – The fae version of "amen."

Airmed – Famous Ancient fae healer, revered as a goddess by some, like so many of the Ancients were. Water fae. Long pale hair, dark eyes.

Alec Ward – Ana's father. Black hair, purple eyes (formerly green and purple, before the Flare). Former Light Guard, now an archeologist hunting Fae Artifacts. Earth Fae, can see in the dark.

Amber Slaight – Former Light Guard, like an aunt to Ana. Eurasian with long dark hair and unique style. Married to Ewan Patterson. Water fae.

Anansanna – The red sun of Aeden at the center of our Earth. Fuels all life on our planet.

Anansanna Alvarsson – AKA Ana. Healer, Water Fae. The second and youngest child of Siri Alvarsson and Alec Ward, both Earth Fae. Female, 19.5 years old. 5'1" with messy chin-length brownish-red hair and green eyes. Named after Anansanna, a fact which she finds embarrassing. Pointy ears. Warm heart, introverted, bumbling and un-coordinated, at least compared to her parents and brother. Hates gym and math, good at writing. Born in late December (Capricorn).

Ancients – Pure-blood fae who lived longer and had stronger powers. Revered as gods by both humans and the newer generations of fae. Few still live today.

Ascensions – Formerly known as Choosings. The ceremony that awakens a faeling's powers on their eighteenth birthday. Before the flare, the ceremony also marked the faeling's alliance with the Light or the Dark.

Aurin – city in Aeden

Ayita – Ana's Fleet.

Bran le Fay – Ana's grandfather, Siri's father. Platinum hair, silver eyes. Earth Fae with special affinity for rocks. Former Commander of the Light Guard. Retired now, enjoying marriage to Frederika Alvarsson.

Brenin Mirro – Well-known artist from Elyiselle, married to Claire Brucie, father of Khai Mirro. Long thin dreads, dark black skin, azure blue eyes.

Cala – A blue grass that has an energizing effect when fae come in contact with it. Grown indoor as carpeting in many fae homes, also harvested to use as a rejuvenating juice or milk.

Chat – Flesh colored communications piece designed to rest in your ear, allowing you talk with anyone, anywhere, anytime. Also works holographically for video-communications.

Claire Brucie – Hollis Mirro's mother and Siri's best friend from childhood. Dark curly hair, often sporting colored streaks. Fire Fae. Brucie means forest sprite in French.

Clarise – David Montauk's cousin who went missing hiking the Long Trail. Tall, blonde.

Cliff Collet – Director of the Montreal Gregor offices. Grammer/Glammer.

Dark Fae – AKA Shades, because there is no true dark, only shades of gray. Fae who believed that humans were a lesser race to be used and ruled. Transformed and reformed thanks to Siri Alvarsson in the Inner Origins series.

David Montauk – 29 year old Starseed, searching for his cousin who went missing on the Long Trail. Blonde hair that is long enough to get into eyes, at least in the front. Brown eyes. No siblings. Traveler.

Dorian Claffsson – Non-nonsense Commander of the Light Guard. Blonde, hazel eyes.

Eastie – A high-speed rail system that connects all the major cities along the Eastern States

Elaine Carhartt– Warper Speaker. Curvy build with long silvery hair. Loves to wear white. Dated Marcus

Riley Cougan —One of David's trail mates, a warper and a friend of Tom. Black hair, blue eyes. Dark Irish. Ellen – leader of camp in woods.

Elsa – Colleague of Siri and Alec that finds golden tablets with writing in Capidocchia, translated in Sumerian for Utu.

Elysielle – Artist enclave in Aeden, Shakespeare and Lennon were from there.

Ewan Patterson – Former Light Guard. Tall, lumberjack-looking fae with red hair. Fire Fae. Married to Amber.

Fae – The original creators of planet earth, origins of all fairy myths and legends of the gods.

Farrah Ward – Ana's aunt who was killed as a child during the war with the Dark. Was six, three years younger than Alec, when she died.

Flare – Inner-earth event thirty years earlier when Siri Alvarsson awakened the Tree of Life in Aeden and amped up Anansanna, releasing a flare of light and ions that changed humans and fae forever. Hate fled the world and love rushed in, catalyzing the utopic reality that Ana currently lives in. Wars ended. Technologies shifted. Humans began evolving fae-like qualities.

Fleet – Unicorn-like white horses with horns and manes that fade to black. Built more like ancient horses – heavy bodies, larger heads and huge, prismed, emerald-green eyes. Communicate telepathically with those that can hear them, and will bond with one rider for life.

Flynn Ward – Alec Ward's Dad. Water Fae, Purple Eyes.

Fredrika Alvarsson – Siri's mother, Ana's grandmother. Auburn hair, hazel eyes. Earth fae.

Gawen Black – Water fae, student at McGill, tall, fine and fair with silver eyes. Two years older than Ana, lives on second floor of Jules' apartment building with Reenah. Plays water polo.

Gladiolus essence – Amplifies connection to Anansanna and boosts powers.

Glima –Viking hand to hand style of combat, working much like Krav Maga to get opponent disarmed and on the ground. Used by many fae warriors.

Grammers – AKA Glammers. Starseeds with the ability to glamour appearance and create illusions. Solar.

Gregors – Watcher organization that oversees the training and well-being of starseeds. Run jointly by humans and starseeds.

Gregory Bank – Huge multinational investment bank. Front for the Gregors.

Grey – Warper prisoner. A grizzled, grey-haired man.

GrounSoft – Durable, weather-proof natural synthetic that has the same sort of give to it as a thick bed of moss.

Used for range of items, from bus seats to bathroom floors.

Hollis Ward – The oldest child of Siri Alvarsson and Alec Ward. Male. Black hair, silvery grey eyes. 23. Infinitely capable and condescending to his sister. Earth fae. Can talk to animals and gets Visions, hard to surprise. Attends Mcgill University and works in student bookstore. Has silver convertible named Miranda.

Jade Alvarsson – Ana's great-grandmother. "Aunt" Jade. Classy, vivacious, looks fifty, dark hair with one white shock over temple. Lives by Lough Ramor in Ireland, west of Dublin. Earth fae.

Jules Harrison – Ana Alvarsson's best friend since grade school, her polar opposite. Tall, skinny, dark as night, and a natural athlete. Great at math. Confident and zany, shy around Hollis who she has a crush on. Birthday in December, just before Ana, making her a Sagittarius. Attending 6-week summer soccer camp at McGill University before the fall.

Kaletka – Siri Alvarsson's Fleet. In Hopi, name means "guardian of the people."

Khai Mirro – Brenin Mirro & Claire Brucie's son, 21.5 years old. Brazilian/latin looking with blue eyes, dark skin. Khai is an Egyptian name, from Claire's time there as a child, meaning "Crowned." Left eyebrow lowers when he doesn't like something.

Lasair – The quick, dance-like martial arts style of the Light Guard. Master this and be a lasrach warrior. Name comes from old Irish word meaning for Flash or Burst of Light

Lifters – Starseeds with the power of telekinesis. Solar.

Light Fae – Light Fae who connect fully with their true nature as fae, the power of Anansanna and the Light.

Respectful of nature and all Earth's creatures, including humanity.

Light Council – The ruling body of the Fae, a council of powerful families and elders.

Light Guard – Elite warriors whose original function was to guard the Light Council. Formerly Aeden's first line of defense against the Dark Fae.

Long Trail – Long-distance hiking trail in Vermont, running the 272-miles through state. The oldest long-distance path in the former United States, now connects to Quebec through Canada.

Lochstuppa – A fae herb that promotes inner peace.

Marcus – Montreal Starseed. Dated Elaine.

Mialloch Airron – Member of the Light Council, the governing body of the fae. Grandson of Airmed, a famous Ancient fae healer. Fastidious. Serious. Brown Hair. Brown Eyes. Air Fae. Taller than Alec by a few inches. Godfather to Ana.

Moonshadow – Alec Ward's Fleet.

Niflhelf – Mountain ranges with portal that accesses the forest north of Montreal.

Nommo – Alien race that traveled to earth and bred with humans, creating the star children or starseeds. Their offspring are aligned with the sun or the moon, awakening with abilities after their 28th birthday when exposed to lunar or solar eclipse events.

North American States – A trading nation comprised of every former country from Panama to Canada, plus Greenland

Popigai Crater – Located in Siberia, the carbon-rich site hold diamonds and meteoric remnants scattered over a 62 mile wide site.

Readers – Starseeds with the power of telepathy. Lunar.

Reenah Shin – Air fae, Gawen's roommate, one year younger than Gawen/year older than Ana. Dark hair, charcoal eyes, eyebrow ring. Asian, tall and slim.

Rose David – Druid/Human female. Red hair, funky dresser, avid snowboarder. Close friend to Siri. Married to Maris (same-sex). Works as a country vet and has a knack for herbalism.

Roumkivara – Region famous for their elite horsemen who ride the Fleet.

Ruis – Hollis Ward's Fleet.

Sasha – Montreal Starseed, Elaine's former mentor.

School – Now, all children of earth receive formal schooling for 14 years, from age 5 to 19, and attend free 7-year college programs.

Shania – Ana & Jules friend from high school.

Sibollae – City in Aeden.

Sienna Cree – Suki Cree's older sister, another girl that likes Hollis.

Siri Alvarsson – Heroine of the Inner Origins series and mother of Ana. Siri means "Marvelous Victory", and Alvarsson means "Elven warrior". Wheaten hair, curly. Tall, thin and fit. Silver eyes. Born in January, Aquarius. Through her Great-grandmother, Morgaine Le Fay, a water fae, she has the ability to heal and to manipulate fate. Through her ancestor Skuld Norna she can see and affect the future, and through the Tyr bloodline, she is honorable and brave, and has the uncanny ability to decide battles. Now an archeologist hunting Fae artifacts with her husband. Earth Fae who can talk to animals.

Speakers – AKA Bards. Starseeds with the power to control minds mind through speech. Solar.

Starseeds – AKA Star Children. Human/alien hybrids with psychic powers.

Suki Cree – Ana & Jules friend from high school, graduation party host.

Tenzin – Warper prisoner.

Tom – Skinny, Asian. Boyfriend of Clarise. Missing.

Travelers – AKA Walkers or Journeyers. Starseeds with the ability to astral travel and navigate dreams. Lunar.

Tree of Life – Massive ancient tree, almost 1000 feet tall and 144 feet in diameter. The origin of all life on earth, powered by the fusion energy of Anansanna.

Valhalla – the capitol city of Aeden, home of the Tree of Life, the Light Council and the Light Guard.

Warpers – Starseeds who use their abilities negatively for personal gain and/or entertainment, regardless of who it hurts. Unaffected by the Flare.

THANK YOU!

We hope you enjoyed book two in the Full Disclosure series. Don't forget to leave a quick review somewhere like Goodreads or Amazon – it's the best way to help support your favorite authors.

Want to See How It All Began?

Discover what it was like to be a Starseed before the world changed – start reading **Song Walker**, the first book in the *Starseeds* series.

Or, check out **Shades of Valhalla**, Book One in the *Inner Origins* Series, and meet Siri and Alec before they saved the world.

About the Author

Ellis Logan lives a quiet life in New England, obsessing daily over superheros and the gods of old. She spends her days corralling wild children and communing with fairies. When everyone is settled down and the owls begin to sing, you'll find her typing away and munching on dark chocolate while unseen spirits whisper stories in her ear.

Follow Ellis on Facebook and Twitter at
EllisLoganBooks

Join Ellis's mailing list at EllisLogan.com
to stay tuned for new releases, giveaways
and more!